Near-Life Experiences

Near-Life Experiences

The Pillow Writers Anthology

Issue 2

Fall 2025

Ann Greenberger, Editor

© 2025 Pillow Writers

Reprinted with corrections

ISBN 9798298682237

All rights reserved. No part of this publication may be reproduced, distributed or transmitted in any form or by any means, including photocopying, recording or other electronic or mechanical methods, without the prior written permission of the publisher, except in the case of brief quotations embodied in critical reviews and certain other noncommercial uses permitted by copyright law. For permission requests, contact Bobbi Ausubel at bobbi.advocate@meaction.net.

Issue 2

Editor: Ann Greenberger

Assistant Editors: Karen Edmonds and Laila Solaris

Cover design: Carmencita Lozano

Cover art: "Poppies" by Laurence Brangea

Profits from the sale of this book benefit #MEAction, meaction.net.

Views expressed in this book are those of the contributors and are not necessarily shared by #MEAction.

Cover description: Watercolor painting of three rosy poppy flowers with petals laid flat and with slender black stems.

Contents

About the Pillow Writers   vii
Foreword   ix
Acknowledgments   xi
A Note from the Editor   xii

iliana pagán teitelbaum
Covidian Fortune   1

Sue Armstrong
Photosynthesis (3:24 a.m.)   3
Moments and Seasons   3

Kathrin H.
Raw Milk   7
Lucky to Have You   8
Show and Tell   9

Stoo Brown
Jonah   11
Not Today   14
Measure My Life   15

Juliet Hattersley
It's cold in the house   17
Last gasp of summer   17
Clear drops of rain   17
Huddling in my blankets   17

Una Hearne
I'm Taking This Lying Down   19
Ghost Girl Believes   21

Jennifer K.
Drift   26

Ethan K.
A Caregiver's Perspective   28

Gail McGinnes
Chronically Normal   30

Michelle Straw
Things That Help Me Breathe   33
As I Walked Out   33
Resonance   34

Laila Solaris
This Rap Is Chronic   36
The Color Orange   37

Dawn McReynolds
Just Make Some Art   41
Becoming Better   41

Kelly Littrell
I Fit Here   43
Sun and Moon   43
Calvin the Dog   45

Martin Keogh
It's Like Amnesia   48
This Long-Haul Illness   48
I Know I   49

Trish Loehrer
To the Caterpillar   51
Rest in Pieces (a Dialogue) 52

Jenny M.
The Endless Wait   56

M. S. Marquart
My Local Life   58
The Bench   59
Power   61

Mary Quigley McGowan
Elizabeth   63
How Are You Feeling?   65

Sarah Sundermeyer
What I (Almost) Tell My Friends   67

Mary Gessert
Robin's Only Desire   68
The Party   69
The Battery   70

Manu Vargas Fernández
The Angry Dog   72
Who You Are   73

Gloria Lucía Fernández Gutierrez
Here and Now   76

Sol Howard
Ten Haiku   79
More   80

CJ Janzen
A Hero's Journey   83
Choose to Live Joyously Within the Tempest of Adversity   86

Emily Wright
Dizzy Girls   89

Emma Parsons
The Inn at Lathones   91

Monique S. Simón
If I Open My Eyes   100
Beauty Struck   101
Clean Linens   101

Emrrys Oliver
I've Been Distant   103
To Be Recited   104
You're There   105

About the Pillow Writers

Who Are the Pillow Writers?

The Pillow Writers is a group of international writers with myalgic encephalomyelitis/chronic fatigue syndrome (ME/CFS) and/or long COVID. The group has met online every Thursday for three years to share their writing and to receive feedback and support. Most participants found this group through friends or the #MEAction website. Anyone with ME/CFS and/or long COVID is welcome to join the Pillow Writers meetings.

There are one hundred Pillow Writers on the email listserv. Currently, there are about twenty participants at meetings each week. Some are experienced writers, and some are new to writing. Writers in this anthology live in the United States, the United Kingdom, Switzerland, France, Colombia, Canada, Ireland, and Scotland. The community of Pillow Writers is growing. Along with the Standard Pillow Writers, additional groups have formed: the Annex for longer works, Soft Pillows for more gentle writings, What Is ME Like? (WIMEL) for nonfiction essays, Early Pillow Writers for Europeans, and Pillow Writers en español for written works in Spanish. For more information on these groups, please visit pillowwriters.wordpress.com.

The Origin of *Near-Life Experiences: The Pillow Writers Anthology*

This literary journal grew out of the Pillow Writers' Thursday meetings and is published annually. Rivka Solomon, ME advocate, invented the name as she thought of the writers who often come to meetings propped up with pillows, in bed, or resting on a couch. Pillow Writer Una Hearne created the term "near-life experiences" and offered it as the title of this anthology.

The Pillow Writers wanted their work available to the broader ME/CFS and long COVID community, and to bring awareness to the general public. The writers in *Near-Life Experiences* open their lives to readers about living with debilitating chronic illness—lives that are rarely seen or understood. The writings here reveal great powers of observation, deep empathy, and joy.

The international advocacy organization #MEAction publicizes and distributes notices about *Near-Life Experiences* to their mailing list of approximately twenty thousand people. Their list includes medical professionals, researchers, disability activists, and family and friends of people with ME/CFS and long COVID. The word is getting out, providing more visibility and more understanding.

What Is ME/CFS?

ME/CFS is a multisystem neuroimmune disease that prevents those affected from engaging in daily activities. Symptoms include difficulty thinking, severe weakness, fatigue, dizziness and chronic pain. After a period of exertion, people may need bed rest for days. Daily tasks like showering, cooking a meal or talking on the phone can be difficult. In the United States, there are more than three million people diagnosed with ME/CFS and twenty million diagnosed with long COVID.[1] Worldwide, more than twenty million people are diagnosed with ME/CFS.[2] At this time, there is no approved treatment or cure. For more information, please visit cdc.gov/me-cfs/about/index.html.

#MEAction and #MillionsMissing

The nonprofit #MEAction is an advocacy group dedicated to people with ME/CFS and long COVID. #MEAction is a beacon of light that people with ME/CFS or long COVID go to for all things related to their condition. They build awareness and power to achieve effective and well-funded research, treatment, care and support.

#MEAction Network's global campaign, #MillionsMissing, advocates for health equity for people with ME/CFS and long COVID. The #MillionsMissing campaign is held annually on May 12. It acknowledges that the people most affected by these diseases are invisible and marginalized. #MillionsMissing demands equality for all people with ME who have been stigmatized and ostracized from healthcare and support.

---

[1] "Clinical Overview of ME/CFS," Centers for Disease Control and Prevention, accessed February 25, 2025, cdc.gov/me-cfs/hcp/clinical-overview; "Long COVID Keeps People Out of Work and Hurts the Economy," Yale Medicine, accessed February 25, 2025, yalemedicine.org.

[2] "Prevalence of Myalgic Encephalomyelitis and Chronic Fatigue Syndrome," #MEAction, accessed February 25, 2025, meaction.net.

Foreword

I am a healthy outsider, the parent of a daughter who has been struggling with ME/CFS for more than thirty years. I am also the cofounder of the Pillow Writers along with Linda Carter. It is a pleasure I never expected. The group was hatched when Zoom became popular during COVID, and so many people were isolated at home, needing to connect with each other. My daughter and I had a conversation one day about relieving the isolation of people with ME/CFS by creating an online writing group. So here we are, three years later.

The writings in *Near-Life Experiences* all originated in the Pillow Writers meetings. What happens in a Pillow Writers meeting? At the beginning, screens appear, lighting up one by one as everyone arrives. People are in chairs or on beds with pillows behind them; some are lying in bed with their cats. Some screens are black or show only a still photo. Those folks may be light sensitive and watching the screen lights hurts them, a symptom of these illnesses. There is the immediate delight of camaraderie. People wave and exchange warm smiles. Most have shown up before, maybe many times. There are usually twenty writers, and often two or three are newcomers. They range in age from eighteen to eighty-five. To me, it feels like a community of friends who see each other's souls.

Chatting begins with a few administrative details. How is the anthology progressing? Are there any volunteers to read their work for an upcoming live online salon?

As the host, I begin by asking, "Who would like to read today?" This is where the group energy leaps forward. Then the readings begin, and people share comments on the readings. This part is a deliciousness of the mind and spirit that I hope you, too, will enjoy as you read the collection of writings in this issue.

I wonder if I can find the language to describe what happens next. A participant offers to read their work (maybe an unfinished work), questions whether it is a worthy piece, and then this vulnerable voice, an authentic voice, seems to reach down into the writer's deep interior being, and images slide forth. They fill me, the listener. Writers read their work twice if it's a poem. Once if it's a longer piece. For me, what happens is that my body center slides upward inside me. Seems to fill my chest, my heart. I am at a different level of consciousness. An unsolicited smile appears on my face. Is it possible I hear the words with my heart? This group has given so much to me that I didn't expect.

Writers offer a collection of words, meanings or images. Cadences, words and accents are Scottish, Irish or British. Maybe a French accent from Switzerland or France, a Spanish accent from Colombia, or regional accents from areas across the United States. There are a variety of genders present. You would not believe all the ways people experience ME/CFS and long COVID, losses and limitations, humor and spiritual growth. Many pieces are not about the illness. These deep dives fill me. Laughter comes easily. Sometimes silence. Maybe four readers take the stage. Plus, there are juicy nonjudgmental comments and critical feedback. They recognize each other's life experience as expressed through their art, their writing. The need is great. They recognize each other as sharing something profound that others rarely understand. This anthology offers the wider world a step into their lives for a moment—to be privy to what few people understand about their lives and to be witness to these powerful accounts.

This social interaction enriches the readings, and the hour and a half is over too quickly. At the close, the group suggests a couple of writing prompts. Come again next week. Then, there are goodbyes. The screen turns dark. My heart feels light. I am reminded each week how beautiful people are. This holds me in the dark times. Those in the group having near-life experiences may tell a different story about what the gatherings mean to them.

I ask myself, what makes this group have no power fights as decisions are being made? Why do people listen to each other so well when they disagree, without blaming or dismissing others' views? I can't answer these questions, but it has something to do with the felt sense that they share something so unique and that they see each other's true selves. They value the chance to bring their experiences, integrity and joy; to be truly seen by others just like themselves in this writing community; to be less isolated; and to be understood.

Enjoy the writings in this issue and see what the poems, stories and essays bring to your heart and your understanding.

Bobbi Ausubel
March 2025

Acknowledgments

First, our gratitude goes to Bobbi Ausubel, who originated the Pillow Writers writing group and facilitates each meeting with wisdom, leadership and compassion. Without her, there would never have been a Pillow Writers group. We just can't imagine that.

To the generous individuals in Pillow Writers who volunteered their time to bring this issue to life, thank you. Laila Solaris managed many rounds of correspondence with authors and brought her artistic eye and clarity to endless decision-making meetings. Stoo Brown provided support for publishing with Kindle Direct Publishing and was always there when called. Juliet Hattersley proofread the final manuscript.

Several volunteers for this issue are not Pillow Writers. They saw the value in *Near-Life Experiences* and offered their time and expertise. Karen Edmonds's superb organizational skills made everything move more quickly. Karen documented the complex editorial and production process to be used for future issues. She offered her professional perspective, volunteered two hundred hours and handled every new challenge with grace and intelligence.

Several professionals volunteered their time and expertise for the cover and interior design. Carmencita Lorenzo created a beautiful cover, and Leslie Eliel provided invaluable final touches. Publishing consultant Mi Ae Lipe advised on how to prepare an interior design that is readable and professional. Jan Innes, a book compositor, assisted with several drafts of the cover and interior. Thank you for caring about this project.

Erin Roediger, programs and campaigns director at #MEAction, provides the internet platform for Pillow Writer meetings. She also organizes multiple publicity efforts for the anthology, giving us visibility on the #MEAction site and sending anthology information to their email list. #MEAction hosts a live reading—a salon—for each issue of the anthology, which means so much to this community. Thank you, Erin, for getting the word out about *Near-Life Experiences*.

To all the Pillow Writers who contributed to this issue, thank you for entrusting your precious, wild and soulful writing to the editors of *Near-Life Experiences*.

A Note from the Editor

Welcome to the second issue of *Near-Life Experiences: The Pillow Writers Anthology*. It took hundreds of volunteer hours to create this issue with twenty-eight Pillow Writer authors and more than one hundred pages. We are growing, with enthusiasm and commitment.

This anthology is a testament to what can be done with the gifts of compassion, intelligence, and endurance from this community of people with ME/CFS and long COVID. There is a great desire for connection among people with invisible disabilities. The rest of the world rarely sees us and often finds these invisible illnesses difficult to understand. Through the intimate writing about our lives, we want you to truly see us. We are confident that *Near-Life Experiences, Issue 2* will offer readers clarity and a deeper understanding of not only who we are but what the world looks like from a perspective that is relatively unknown to those outside of our community.

For this issue, we edited each piece, designed an interior that is clean and easy to read, and included new features. There are two essays by the family of people with ME/CFS. Gloria wrote about her daughter (Pillow Writer Manu) moving back home, and Pillow Writer Jennifer's son wrote about having a mother with ME/CFS. Also, new to this issue, we added photos to the contributors' notes so that readers can see who we are. It is remarkable to read the notes and see the breadth of this group of writers—the countries where they live, the careers they once had and their current circumstances. I hope you enjoy this broad cross section of talent, intelligence and world views that come together in this issue.

Join me in celebrating these talented writers and discovering their worlds.

Ann Greenberger, MFA
August 2025

iliana pagán teitelbaum

Covidian Fortune

I woke up
looking for my good fortune,
as I did every morning.
But yet again, it seems
I have misplaced it.

Perhaps under the bed,
together with my ability to
walk around the block?
Or in the closet, with the
work clothes I no longer wear?
Or the drawer, with the keys to the
car I can no longer drive?
Or the overflowing laundry basket, along with the
energy to do everyday chores?
Or the toilet, with my ability to
get out of bed?
Or in the backyard, buried like the
bone of my old friendships?

I look under the covers.
My chest rises and falls erratically.
There it is!
Transparent as the air
I try so hard to breathe
or the dogged glow around
my earthly form.
There I am!
(As my father said softly on the phone
the month before he passed,
aquí estoy todavía.)

Here I am!
Rushing through space
at more than 100,000
kilometers per hour
on a pine and cotton bed
tied to my huge round vessel
by an undetectable force that keeps
all the earth, air, and water
that my fellow navigators and I need
for the journey.

There I go
Soft as a snail, swift
as a shooting star.
My continued existence in this
darling ephemeral body is the
only proof of my
good fortune.
And there it was,
under the covers
all along!

iliana pagán teitelbaum is a Puerto Rican educator and filmmaker. She researches media and inequality in Latin America and the Caribbean. She is disabled by long COVID and is passionate about disability justice.

Sue Armstrong

Photosynthesis (3:24 a.m.)

Let spring in
through this open window
and let wildflowers
find fertile ground
in this mattress
as my winter self decays

Let in sunlight and warm rain
so these wild flowers
photosynthesize
and fill this stagnant room
with oxygen
so that I may breathe
again

Moments and Seasons

the air is heavy tonight
warm and clinging to my skin
thick in my lungs

too hot outdoors
I go inside
to wait
for the storm

lightning flashes
in the darkening sky
thunder rumbles

the sky releases
rain pours
on the rooftop
and the garden

it quiets and slows
the worst of it passed
the storm now tracking eastward
along the lake
to you

and you,
no stranger to storms
that rage inside
with slow, quiet devastation,
welcome it
this storm

its bold declaration
the speed with which it passes
how it washes things clean
and cools the air

I think of you
and how through all of our storms
and all of these years
we have had each other

shelter
constant
strong and steady

moments and seasons
of words that didn't need to be spoken
and words that always could be
of love and life
late nights and laughter

what an unexpected rainbow, you
your light refracted
through the rains of these last ten years
into so many beautiful colours

when I think of you leaving
I think about light
how it can be reflected or absorbed
and I know that you will never really be gone

we will all, both carry it within us
and reflect it outward into the world
all that you have given us
the light that you've shared

and when that day comes
your storms here finished
our moments and seasons done
I will go outside
when the air is heavy
to the garden
to wait

to find you there
amidst the lightning
in all of its incredible fierceness
and in the quiet aftermath
of the storm
with dark clouds, sunlight
and the beauty
of rainbows

 **Sue Armstrong** lives in Ontario, Canada. She has been living with ME for more than ten years and began writing in 2024. Her poem "Moments and Seasons" is dedicated to her dear friend Jeff. In addition to being a wonderful friend, Jeff has been instrumental in furthering understanding and knowledge of ME in Canada through his work with Millions Missing Canada.

Kathrin H.

Raw Milk

My mum sends me to the farmer at the end of the street. It's not far. I'm a big girl. I can do it. I get to take the milk can with the lid. It's a serious object, not a toy. Its shiny stainless steel is cold to the touch. I can sway it by the wooden handle like a basket. I'm fascinated. Fill it with three litres, mum says. She shows me the mark and lets me repeat: How much? Three litres, I say, earnestly feeling the wooden handle in one hand and the cold, big coin in the other.

I love the milk can. It looks a bit like the big churns the farmer uses to send milk to the dairy farther up the village. But those are huge, heavy things. To move them he rolls them over their bottom rim, slightly tilted to one side because they are too heavy to lift with their forty litres of milk inside. It's a delicate balance, strange looking in the big, rough, red hands of the farmer. It seems like a dance: light and easy, but I get that it is a hard thing, a practice thing. I know all about practice things because I'm the youngest. Everyone else has more practice. They can do stuff, but I need practice. For example, my big brother says, if you swing our milk can fast enough in a big upright circle from toe to head to toe, fast fast fast, nothing will fall out. He dares me to try it with the filled milk can—no lid needed, promise! I won't, because I'm not stupid. I'm undecided if it's doable and I need practice or if he is lying and just being mean. Off you go! My mum stops my musings about the gravity of milk and the untrustworthiness of elder brothers.

I smell the farm before I reach it. Warm milk, cow dung, hay and fumes from the tractor. It's a good mix, full of life. I'm happy there, but today I'm a lot more: proud, scared, shy and confident. Three litres please, I interrupt the farmer with outstretched hands, coin in one, pot in the other. He takes the can but gives me back the coin: pay when you get the goods.

While I wait for him, I suddenly realize there are calves, right there. They moo and stretch their heads out of the little opening of the shed. Five, six curious, gangly calves. I'm in heaven. There is a dare I will do and have done before: I carefully put the coin into my dungarees and hold my hands in front of the moist snouts. In seconds my fingers disappear in a warm, wet suckling tunnel. The calves are gentle but forceful. Rough scratchy tongues and yes, teeth are now wrapped around my fingers and hands. I have to hold firmly against them, or they will surely swallow me whole. It is, after all, a dare! I giggle, sharing a scared, happy, hyped, wonderful moment with the calves—while we all wait for milk.

Lucky to Have You

I'm lucky to have you. I wish that I could say, I'm lucky to have you just because you are kind, open-minded and curious. Because of your sharp, sparkly mind and a really good body. Because of your sweet eyes and the big, big heart. Because you're funny, never mind the horrible dad jokes, which make me laugh against my will. I'm lucky to have you because of how you see the world and because of your values, which are as kind as you are and haven't become more conservative even though we're at that age where everyone says they will. I'm lucky to have you because you bring chaos in my otherwise too neat world and challenge me all the time to be kinder and weirder.

I wish that were why I told people, I'm lucky to have you. But instead, I talk about how you stayed when my sickness started to disrupt our world and even when it started to dominate it. I tell them how I simply couldn't do without you.

You fetch and you carry—I wish it were beers on a hot summer's night or a backpack while we travelled. But instead, it's tea, yet another cushion, and that cold pack from the freezer for my aching whatever body part.

You hope with me, try another new thing with me and you're crushed with me when it eventually fails. You hold my hand, endure my rage and dry my tears. I too do the hand holding, the comforting, the dreaming and talking—of that, I do the majority. But the roles are set. I need and you give—that is what people see.

I'm lucky to have you because after long days at work you cook, you tidy up, you clean—while I watch and tell you where you missed a spot. Yes, I'm very popular these days. You pack my bags when we try against our better judgement to go on holiday, so that I can lie in another bed with another view and with more symptoms after the journey. You push me in my wheelchair because the electric one is still not here. You sit on my bedside, showing me pictures from the outside and telling me stories from your day. They are too long, and you mess up the endings—but I love them.

I'm lucky to have you because you stayed when I got too ill to work. You're paying for everything now. Fuck disability in Switzerland. I'm scared to be so dependent on you. You're scared, too. We both felt a little trapped—how could we ever break up in this situation? We hope it holds. Yet we gave each other permission to leave should we need to. That is the strange, beautiful love declaration of an inter-abled couple.

There are still a lot of things that mostly I do. I'm the analyst, the organizer, the travel agent, sometimes the therapist and all the time the online shopper of our little operation. I'm the brain and you are the muscle—it's an old joke, but nowadays it's not funny anymore. I simply could not manage without help, and I am beyond grateful that it comes from you.

Show and Tell

Show me your messy bedhead, the pile of books unread
Show me your pale faces, your crinkly pillows' cases
Baby plant on windowsill, the latest let's-try-this-pill
Some new pajamas—wait, are those llamas?

What of the latest dismissal, the one that made you bristle?
Tell me of nightmares, tell me who really cares
Tell me who you miss the most, which conversations you ghost

Show me rings under your eyes, hearts longing for open skies
Show me holes in your speech, all you want are waves . . . the beach
Dust piles on a late hobby, this all started with Bobbi
Glitter stickers on a cane, never in the fast lane

What makes you tick, your tired synapses click?
Tell me of your newest passion, oh yes, you will need to ration
Tell me of the online course, you're an unstoppable force

Show me your reason for joy, a story with the word *ahoy*
Show me where you find hope, how the fuck do we cope?
Positivity like a bubble tea, love as vast as the blue-green sea
A screen full of kind faces, your words taking us places

Give me an island to swim to. Some rest from this forever flu.
Unattainable ways of life surrounding me,
Comparison incessant like a cold grim sea.
Give me an island to swim to. Belonging, a warm happy glue.

Kathrin H. is a queer intersectional feminist who has had ME for more than a decade. She lives with her husband in Zürich, Switzerland. Stories, written or spoken, are her thing. Be they movies, novels, poems or spoken word art—they all make her small world bigger. As does writing. During her career in public relations and while studying journalism and communications, writing was a central part of her professional self. Before ME fully took over, she loved to cycle, swim, hike, run—anything active outdoors. Housebound, she now enjoys whatever green she can catch from her balcony, where she is a forty-two-year-old in full-on granny mode watching birds and bugs. Formerly fiercely independent and restless, ME has taught her to ask for and accept help, to pause, to let go and not to compare.

Stoo Brown

Jonah

> *Now the Lord had prepared a great fish to swallow up Jonah. And Jonah was in the belly of the fish three days and three nights.*
>
> Jonah 1:17, King James Version

"I was Jonah," said Brent.

He said it with conviction, with sincerity, but he said it gruffly because that was his way. He was in no way a refined man, nor a polished orator, but he held the room. His right hand twisted the buttons on his pea coat. In his left hand was his Bible, not open but closed. He didn't need to open it—he knew the words by heart.

"And you, brothers and sisters; you were the great fish sent by the Lord."

The congregation responded, "Amen, Brother Brent." They saw the story of his salvation in exactly the same terms.

Brent had been born and raised on the west coast island of Harris, in the town of Stornoway, a son, grandson and great grandson of fishermen and equally a son, grandson and great grandson of kirkmen. The Free Kirk's fierce dogma on right and wrong had been drilled—and occasionally beaten—into him from birth, but it carried not enough influence to protect him from family tragedies in youth whose miseries were multiplied tenfold by alcohol in adulthood. Eventually, a friendless, foundering hulk, faced with a lee-shore and almost certain destruction, he had been rescued by his brethren in the kirk at his darkest hour and, over many difficult months, had been strictly remade into the man who now stood, sober and intense, in God's House.

Once he'd returned to the straight and narrow—very narrow— path, Brent had rekindled his father's conviction that there was no point in reading the Good Book if you didn't also live by it, and the extremity of his fall, followed by the labours of his rescue, had anchored that conviction still more deeply. Consequently, when faced with the dilemma of where to live, he chose an abandoned but spacious sailmaker's shed, seeing no need for anything more comfortable.

"Ye cannae bide here!" said Angus, the social worker sent to check up on him. "Fer a start, it's no' taxable as a residential property."

"If it's the tax ye're efter, I'll willingly pay," responded Brent, unperturbed. "'Render therefore unto Caesar the things which are Caesar's.'" For Brent the words of Jesus were sufficient answer.

"No, no, Brent, it's no' the tax," protested Angus with emphasis. Tax was a subject he wished to stay well away from and he regretted even mentioning it. "It's gey cauld and damp. It'll no be guid fer yer health."

In any other person an ironic laugh might have been forthcoming. Brent just smiled, his mouth barely visible behind his dense grey beard.

"Aye, an' it's gey cauld and damp oot there oan a fishing boat. If I cannae bide here then jist put me doon as 'homeless.'"

"I cannae dae that either," responded Angus, frustrated.

"'Foxes ha'e holes, and the birds o' the air ha'e nests; but the Son o' Man hath nowhere to lay his heid.' I'll jist bide here: dinnae ye fash aboot me."

And so it was settled: Brent lived in the sailmaker's shed and Angus didn't think any more about it.

And then there was the matter of employment. Hard work was a virtue; sloth was most definitely a vice. There were only two things that Brent knew—fishing boats and drinking—and he put his knowledge of both to good use. Monday to Saturday he worked at the harbour and the boatyards, taking any job he was given and making an honest wage. At three on Friday and Saturday afternoons he'd finish whatever he was doing, clean his shed, lay out some bedding and wait. Very quickly the local drunks discovered that a basic bed, a hot bath and a solid breakfast were available at the sailmaker's shed after closing time and no questions were asked. The police learnt fast, too, and took advantage—placing an inebriated detainee with Brent was easier than holding them in cells. There were never very many— never more than four or five on a Saturday night—but there was always someone. Only three obligations were placed on the patrons of the shed: They brought no alcohol in; they had to be out by nine o'clock, rain or shine; and, as they departed, they had to accept the blessing "Go ye in peace and sin no more."

The kirk, quietly and discreetly, approved of Brent's work. It was, they felt, the work of the Lord. And if Brent did it, then that meant they didn't have to. He never asked for any money but neither did he have to pay any rent: The kirk took care of that. Frequently, plastic bags would be placed in an old bin at the shed's door. Not rubbish being discarded, but anonymous gifts of food and clothing, left for Brent to use in meeting the needs of broken men.

It wasn't just a service to local folk, not by any means. Fishing vessels from many nations—Spain, Ireland, all the Scandinavian and Baltic states—called at Stornoway and their crews would be in need of Brent's care as much as any other. And it was a vessel from Iceland that brought a permanent resident, a female. She was old, certainly not pretty and walked slowly, with a stiff limp, but she had a warm welcome for any friend of Brent's. She rarely used her voice and demanded only simple fare. She slept on his bed and every morning he was awoken by the thump of her tail wagging enthusiastically. No one knew her name, but she came from an Icelandic trawler—of that they were certain—and she simply became known first as "the Iceland dog," then "Iceland," and finally just "Icy."

It sounds noble laid out like this, but in reality, it was not. The shed was cold and drafty, Brent's daytime work was hard and tedious, and the hospitality he offered cost him dearly. Drunk men are all too often violent, intolerant and abusive: Hungover men are rarely grateful. Cleaning up urine, vomit and yes, even faeces was humiliating. And strangely, ordinary, local folk, folk who never sullied their own hands or risked their own reputations, could be coldly critical of those who did good work. But Brent knew all this before he started and he shared his tribulations with his Saviour and with Icy. Far outweighing the difficulties, though, was the net of trust, loyalty and affection which slowly spread around him. Wherever fishing boats went, fishermen would talk of the godly man in the sailmaker's shed in Stornoway, the man with the friendly dog.

Note: Kirk = church; lee-shore = a particular hazard to shipping; gey = very; bide = live; fash = trouble, bother.

Not Today

My mind is naught but banks of fog
circling round a roiling deep,

        purposeless rotation.

My heart is just a space, a void,
hollow cave of emptiness,

        a-beat without sensation.

My rising, falling, painless chest
gathers breath and sends it back,

        monotonous vocation.

There is no poem in me today.

Nothing. Empty. Neutral. Blank.

Measure My Life

Measure my life?
Ten days in the sun?
The five-star penthouse.

A chance hole-in-one?
Bracket: cell: bracket:
Sixteen. Autosum.

Measure my life?
Tell me, pray, why?
Who stands to profit?

With whom do you vie?
Who's doing the counting?
And don't they just lie.

Measure my life?
Don't be absurd.
Oh god, please don't.

Stop.
Wait.

Just hear a word.

Pause. Ponder. Listen.
Tick tock, tip toe.

Pause. Ponder. Listen.
Tick tock, come, go.

Pause. Ponder. Listen.
The blankets, the sheets,
The discarded books, the dull thudding beats.

Don't measure my life,
Not even with sand:

Sit down;

Sit here;

Sit still;

Hold my hand.

Stoo Brown lives in the middle of Scotland with his wife and two cats, and he counts himself lucky to be surrounded by countryside. He is confined to bed, but writing is an activity which ME has not robbed him of, enabling him to roam the world or travel through time. And it was Pillow Writers who made this all possible.

Juliet Hattersley

It's cold in the house.
I open the windows anyway
to smell spring.

Last gasp of summer—
one wrinkled plum.

Clear drops of rain—
Trying not to be depressed,
I gaze at pine branches.

Huddling in my blankets—
Tonight, even the stars
look cold.

Juliet Hattersley has been ill with ME/CFS since at least 1988. She attempts to keep up her spirits with coffee, her partner, her cats, and contact with friends. She joined Pillow Writers last year and is always disappointed when her system is too overloaded to participate. Juliet's blog *Sorta Kinda Haiku* is at sortakindahaiku.blogspot.com. She hopes her writing shows a sense of humor and evolving skill.

Una Hearne

I'm Taking This Lying Down

- Fight your fears.
- She fought a brave battle with cancer.
- They fought for their rights, for justice.
- Push through, drive on.
- They fight for their country, for freedom.
- Fight off infection, never miss a day at work.

The heroic nature of fighting is built into our language and beliefs. Part of being human is the ability and impulse to fight. We are programmed to believe there are winners and losers. Fighters are winners. Choosing not to fight or being unable to is considered weak and even cowardly.

We have wars on drugs, obesity and terrorism. None of which have succeeded in their aims. Interestingly, there is no war on harmful or addictive prescription drugs, junk food, or state control and corruption.

I have ME/CFS (myalgic encephalomyelitis/chronic fatigue syndrome). I am supposed to fight it like a good heroic patient. When I say I am not fighting, I am resting. I hear, "You can't do nothing! You have to try everything! How do you expect to get well if you just give up?"

To be clear, I have not given up. I have learned. The hard way. Fighting this illness is futile and can result in far more serious illness. Along with many others, I have learned that from experience.

Our ancestors knew better. In the absence of drugs or treatments that cure, the traditional treatment for illness was bed rest, good food and fresh air. No overstimulation and certainly no stress.

Before antibiotics, the treatment for tuberculosis was a rest cure in a sanatorium. And if an intervention caused the patient to decline, it was stopped immediately. Common sense. It's a pity it is so uncommon. Stop, rest and allow the body to heal itself as much as possible.

So, for a modern world I have invented a new extreme sport:

Extreme Rest

This is not a sport for the fainthearted. It requires intensive training and development over many years; however, the rewards are also extreme.

There are a few aspects to the training:

- You will need some basic qualifications. PhDs in: Acceptance, Listening to and Understanding your unique body, and Patience.

- Like all extreme sports, mindset is key. You will need to change some of your core, unconscious beliefs to the following:
    - Resting is an important activity and is not laziness.
    - There is no shame in not being able to work or partake in family or social life.
    - Self-flagellation is inappropriate and a massive waste of energy.
    - Being ill is just a thing which happens to humans and is not your fault.

- There are muscles to develop for Extreme Rest and these require daily practice to stay in top condition:
    - Resilience in the face of truths such as "You are still sick and that is OK."
    - Creativity in adapting to the changing or new symptoms and circumstances.

- "Not doing." Restraining yourself daily from doing things—even things you love or think you "should."

The demands of Extreme Rest as a sport are very great. It is not advisable to undertake this sport lightly. Of course, it is not usually a choice. Life chooses you for this sport and you must simply do your best.

There are risks, as with all extreme sports. The main risks are to your mental health and relationships as well as your physical health. It is important to get as much support as possible with all of these. You cannot get to the Olympics without a support team.

Disappointingly, there are no medals or prizes for Extreme Rest. The rewards we train so hard for are stabilization and maybe even improvement. Achievements for our top athletes are measured in small pockets of energy stored up for doing things we love. The pinnacle, the holy grail, if you will, is in avoiding crashing altogether. For me, this is as mythical an aim as finding the holy grail, but fun to aim for.

So, my chosen sport is Extreme Rest. You will have to forgive me for accepting I am ill. Forgive me for not fighting it. Please forgive me for not explaining myself or justifying what I am doing; I cannot spare the energy to educate you. Forgive me, please, for . . .

I am taking this lying down.

Ghost Girl Believes

Yes I will welcome death, because I believe
that dying releases our spirit from our lumpen corpse.
Untethered yet still conscious we are free to wander
we can choose our own direction, set our own sweet course.

No one knows what lies beyond behind the veil.
The wisest man I know told me "We will wait and see." Yes.
Of course. We have no option
we cannot see from here . . .   and yet . . .

I have such time to think, endless hours prone
unable to get up and go—to do the things I wish.
I must lie and wait or lie and wonder.
Because I wonder I shall wander to witness wonder, I'll fly free.

Perhaps hitch a ride on yon eagle's back
survey those yawning landscapes seen only on TV.
The sweep from summit down to valley on an awesome scale
jagged shoulders rock wearing cloaks of deepest snow

or luscious jungle covers, sloping downwards steep enough
to take my breath away. Vast tracts of land to soar o'er
imbibing beauty, majesty, creation,
artistry in every stone, bloom, leaf and feather.   Just for us?

                                                                           Surely not.

If it were just for us, we would be compelled to stop.
And stare. Drink in the glory—we would not return
to mundane lives. We could not. We would instead become
statues, knelt in prayer, planted in the landscape.

In our present form we cannot see feel hear it all.
From universe to atom. From cradle to our grave
we are too small, too blinkered blind distracted
to absorb magnificence on this scale.

Yet we are a conscious part of this
unimaginable tapestry of life. For a time
we wear a body uniquely fashioned
to last our lifetime longing.

Before we came and when we leave
our essence? consciousness? spirit? soul?
Whatsoever name you know it by
lives on—I believe—in an altered form.

Unencumbered by our leaden body suit, our spirit free
to flit and be, anywhere and anywhen. We may
experience anything—at every scale absorb
the breadth and depth and breath of life.

I shall fly o'er rivers as they wind and wend
through plains and valleys, splash with joy
in the thunderous orchestra of waterfalls
dancing with the droplets—no peril for a spirit.

I shall lay upon the furry back of a random butterfly
me so small, its wings a wall, stretching up away.
Surrounded by the scent of flower down below.
Surprise, its wings begin to beat a sound

made out of air. In flight again my spirit soars.
Dazzling kaleidoscope of colours—wings
of my chariot and flowers we alight upon.
To know the taste of nectar via nature's straw.

Exquisite beauty in every wing and petal
which proliferate around the Earth
What need have we of unicorns?
When the every day bewitches.

I shall pass millennia but know not time.
Witness the birth of Earth and know if Darwin's theory stands.
Then watch the spread of us across the globe
it's in our nature to migrate, discovering new lands.

Watch us expand from mud huts to cottages of stone
back when the world was a size that made some sort of sense.
I'll watch us scurry, settle, build, destroy and build again and see
roads crisscross the land like so many painted strips.

I wish to revel in the best of us: love, laughter and
shared life. Witness moments of pure joy—that ignited smile
between two refugee kids in a line—the picture
I have never found again, yet never have forgotten.

I'll sit beside great artists
drinking in each brush stroke
my spirit dancing to the music
my emotions played by words.

Sadly I will also see our fatal flaw in action
as we hate, destroy and decimate—nothing new to us.
But now I'll see it differently I hope I'll see the point,
understanding is the only salve to heal our deepest sorrows.

For respite I will find a squirrel and nestle
on its furry back, cocooned by its unlikely tail.
Such a flaunting of luxury and style! Show off or not,
I shall simply feel the comfort for my soul.

I shall feel the warmth and safety
of its home in scented wood.
Curled around sensational delight
at last I'll rest and rest .... and deeply rest.

I choose to contemplate and further still, believe
this tale which makes me happy for the end. Do
you think I am a fantasist? Delusional? Quite mad?
Perhaps possessed of wisdom maybe? No?

Well, I have one question left I offer simply to
you do not have to answer, take this how you will:
What do you choose to believe, what shapes all you see?

How's that working for you? . . . And is it working still?

 **Una Hearne** lives in Ireland and has been writing all her life, mostly about life and personal development. Since she joined the Pillow Writers, poems keep appearing out the end of her pen. She finds this weird. Having had ME for more than forty years since a bout of mononucleosis at age sixteen, Una is now mostly housebound. She did manage to work for more than twenty years and misses being a life coach and trainer like breathing. She is very glad she can still write and is profoundly grateful to the fabulous Pillow Writers.

The following essay, "Drift" by Jennifer K., explores the depth of the support she receives from her son. An essay by her son, Ethan, follows. He shares what it is like for him to have a mother with ME.

Jennifer K.

Drift

There was no energy for extra movement, so we brought a white inner tube printed with strawberries and tropical fruit. It coordinated with the umbrella and blanket where I lay in a state of repose, absorbing the soothing warmth of sand and the relaxing sound of crashing waves, a few minutes or more.

My son carried the inner tube to the water for me, and I sank my illness into it. I was too ill to swim, so I floated on the inner tube—its buoyancy a mobility aid on water. The Atlantic was warm against our skin, both playful and calm. We could not see the ocean floor though, and when something big and scary brushed my son's side, there was a mingled burst of nervous laughter when we realized the invisible was simply my foot drifting away.

He stayed next to me . . . a comfort in itself. I trusted his care and his carefulness completely. My son, a teenager, yet a man mature in his abilities, observations, and caring. His eyes watching out for me, a hundred times or more.

The inner tube drifted with the current, which was transverse and quite strong. But the current was not as strong as my son. He pulled me protectively back to safety, allowing me to let loose and feel peace and joy in the sensations of float and drift.

He repeated this play of drifting and pulling, floating towards danger then pulling back to safety, a dozen times or more.

It was much akin to his care in my illness, repeatedly pulling me from darkness back to light. He is always there, even when he isn't.

A phone call. A text. An in-person visit. I used to watch over him. Now he watches over me. Pulling me back from illness . . . a million times or more.

Jennifer K. is the mother of Ethan, whose voice is also included in this anthology. Jennifer and Ethan live in the Midwest with their husband/father, dog and two cats. Prior to developing ME and long COVID, Jennifer was an avid sports woman. She played tennis, lifted weights, ran half marathons, and took kickboxing and martial arts classes. She currently enjoys televised football (on good days), sitting in nature on her patio, fresh flowers delivered by loved ones and listening to simple music. Though she had a successful scientific career for twenty-three years, the defining achievement of her life is the close, loving relationship she maintains with her son, who is a most compassionate, caring and supportive young man. Jennifer is grateful to her husband, son, friends, family and the Pillow Writers for their continued grace, support, sharing and encouragement.

The following essay by Ethan K. explores what it is like to have a mother with ME. His mother Jennifer K. wrote "Drift," which is also included in this anthology.

Ethan K.

A Caregiver's Perspective

My mom is one of many people who suffers from ME. Although I do not have the disease, I have witnessed my mom battle through it. Her ME began when I was a freshman in high school. At the time, I did not fully understand what she was going through because I had never heard of ME before. Now I am going into my sophomore year of college, and I have learned much more about the condition.

Obviously, this disease has taken a toll on my mom. Things are not as easy for her as they once were. Trips are harder if she is even capable of going, conversations may be misinterpreted between us, and she can easily be unable to leave the house for a couple of weeks at a time. With that said, I try my best to be around her and brighten her day. I try to come up with activities to do around the house with her, go on short walks, or head into town. I have learned it is important to be patient and considerate when talking to my mom because it gives her time to think and talk with me without being flustered.

My dad is doing a great deal to provide for us with my mom now unemployed. He has his main career along with side jobs that help support us. He is the absolute hardest working person I have ever known. He is around the house after the workday but leaves for work at 7 a.m., which means my mom is at home alone. It is not my dad's fault in any way that she is alone in the daytime, and she knows that, but I always feel bad.

Going to college was tough because I wanted someone to be with my mom. I lived in a dorm on campus. Almost every night, I called her to ask about her day, make plans for the weekend, and talk about our pets. I always thought that helped her, and it helped me as well. The university I attended last year was only twenty-two minutes from my house, so it was easy to have my dad or a friend pick me up and drive me home, or for my mom to visit. Nearly every weekend we did one or the other. It put me at ease that my mom had something to look forward to, that I could visit home, or she could come up. Hanging out with my family is something I always enjoy.

I am grateful for my family and what I have in my life. My mom is the strongest, most determined person I know. I believe there is a future where this disease can be cured. Like everyone who suffers from ME, she deserves to conduct her life at a regular level and not be slowed down by it. I have heard things are trending in a more positive direction regarding the attention ME is getting from doctors and medical experts. I am grateful that is the case, and I hope more awareness is raised with doctors as time goes on.

If you are a person who knows someone struggling with ME, I strongly urge you to spend time with them. It has helped me develop patience, understanding of ME, and better caregiving abilities by being around my mom. I am sure that could be the case for others as well. I understand I will never know what it is like to experience ME, but I can offer love and support to my mom and give her hope. Others who know someone with ME can offer support, too.

———◆———

Ethan K. is a sophomore in college. When not studying, he enjoys football, baseball, basketball and music. He sang and played percussion for six years and is currently teaching himself how to play guitar. Ethan's newest hobby is woodworking, and he recently finished making his first piece of furniture, a bookcase, from scratch. In his freshman year of college, Ethan conducted research on black sand collected from Puerto Rico. During his sophomore year, he intends to advance his background in research. Ethan enjoys playing with his cat and hanging out with his friends and family.

Gail McGinnes

Chronically Normal

The postman comes
I can't get to the door
when visiting the toilet
fatigue means crawling on the floor
I'm so hungry
kitchen's distance seems like miles
place bread in the toaster
then collapse on cold kitchen tiles.

My bloods are normal so you don't hear ME.

Attempt a shower
within seconds I must get out
I lie in a puddle
on the verge of passing out
crawl back to the bedroom
cold, wet, shivering
no energy to dry
laying in my soggy bed quivering.

My bloods are normal so you don't hear ME.

Legs like lead
almost impossible to walk
my brain is mush
can't grasp the words to talk
lights blind me
hurting my head
a previous lover of music
auditory overwhelm now puts me in bed.

My bloods are normal so you don't hear ME.

My vulnerable carcass
reacting to everything I eat

you refer me to dieticians
outside of your office, bum hardly touched the seat
lovely dietician
tries to help, offers her best
she thinks there's something really wrong
says I need more tests.

My bloods are normal so you don't hear ME.

I've been off work
a week, a month, now years
I've lost my health, my job, my home
there's not much left to fear
repeated visits
still no treatment or tonic
been ill so long now
you consider me chronic.

My bloods are normal so you don't hear ME.

Disability equipment for showering
resigned owner of a wheelchair
I'm only in my thirties
life can be so unfair
abandoned by you
aren't doctors supposed to care?
The stress of dealing with them
brings on a symptom flare.

My bloods are normal so you don't hear ME.

A decade on
not much has changed
except me and the doctors
are now estranged
it's mental health teams
I now visit with my woes

that's where you end up
when medically nobody knows.

My bloods are normal so you don't hear ME.

**Gail McGinnes** lives in the west of Scotland with her husband and rescue dog. She was diagnosed with ME/CFS in 2014 after contracting a flu-like virus in 2012, which she never recovered from. Like many with this illness, she is no longer able to work and had to give up her career as an Occupational Therapist in Scotland's National Health Service (NHS).

Gail started journaling in 2017 but found poetry coming out the end of her pen in 2021. This turned out to be a safe way to connect with and express emotions without becoming overwhelmed. She now writes regularly for her own mental and emotional well-being and finds the Pillow Writers group a safe and supportive space to share her writing and experiences of chronic illness.

When she is well enough, Gail also writes, creates and produces yoga nidra meditation audios for the meditation app Insight Timer.

Michelle Straw

Things That Help Me Breathe

The moon
When your fullness
Outshines the streetlamp from my bedroom window.
When your waxing promises
Halt me mid-step to the recycling bin.
When your waning
Slips into my rearview mirror.
I draw breath and release.

The Red Cedar tree
When your needles form a cloak,
A womb,
Hiding your encroach onto a long-forgotten tomb.
When your branches are bare,
Your bark revels in winter.
You draw me close
And as I cling to your expansive breast,
I draw breath and release.

As I Walked Out

As I walked out one August day,
I saw you striding past.
Each foot thud, a pebble in water
Rippled up your barely lycrad flesh.

As I walked out one August day,
I saw you shuffling away from uniformed learning,
Eyes to the floor,
Bulging rucksack clashing against plastic bags on your back,

Clips clacking and toggles jangling against drinks bottles,
Your worldly belongings weighing you down,
A refugee seeking the asylum of a safe home.

And then you stalled.
You faltered at a junction with a waiting car.
I drew up alongside and crossed the road.
You followed in my footsteps,
Safe passage,
Then shuffled ahead,
Eyes down,
Your world on your shoulders.

Resonance

Sometimes a rustling resonates across the room
Responding to the forces of an invisible wave.
It's the same resonance that fills my core,
The sound of the universe.

I look over to the source, a snare drum, and remember
Sticks clasped in hands flirting, flitting, flying,
Feet dancing across pedals,
Synchronous polyrhythms ebbing and flowing,
Maroon lacquered toms drilling and pacing,
With bass booming,
Marking tide and time.

The snare that started it all,
Accents, trills and fills,
Always the show off.

The hi-hat, in perpetual banter with the bass
Counter-balances the clear current of the ride
And is, in turn punctuated,
Now by the splash,

Then by the crash,
In a reverberating wave
That breaks and dissipates
And is no more than a memory.

Michelle Straw lives in South West England. She has published academic writing in linguistics. She also loves playing music, racket sports, skiing and scuba diving. Over the years, she has had to give up most of these activities due to poor health. Since contracting COVID in 2020 and now living with long COVID, she has decided to radically transform her life and develop new passions. She writes poetry and short pieces that provide therapeutic benefit and appreciates the understanding and compassion she receives from fellow Pillow Writers. She is freed from the tyranny of the academic peer review process. Having sold her drum kit, she still plays guitar and hopes to pick up her saxophone again very soon. She is multilingual, so her COVID brain can now forget words in multiple languages.

Laila Solaris

This Rap Is Chronic

This poem is for the spoonies in my tribe,
People who have to suffer, daily, trying to survive.
This poem is for the dreamers on my team,
We all know why the caged bird sings.

I woke up one day, couldn't get out of bed.
Like my body was a car and the battery was dead.
It was like my whole system was just flat out of gas,
My HPA axis wasn't up to the task.

I was stepping on the pedal, couldn't get myself in gear.
I was sick as a dog, I was losing my hair,
I was losing my mind, couldn't put my thoughts together,
My brain slowed down like L.A. traffic in hot weather.

The only thing my mind could focus on was FEAR,
Like a depression insurrection, Yah, you bet I was scared,
Like living in a horror movie that turned out to be real.

I tried everything on God's earth that might help me heal,
Doctors tested my blood, and my sweat, and my tears.
They tried hard to find an answer, the solution was elusive,
When the tests always came back as "inconclusive."

One doctor, 2 doctor, 3 doctor, 4,
I've been to see 27 doctors or more.
I spent my all money, all my spoons, and all my time,
To finally discover that I had Lyme.

And then my doctors gave me antibiotics,
They made me so sick that I wanted narcotics.
Thanks to a thing they call Herxheimer reactions,
When the cure feels worse than the original problem.

There were times when I said *I can't stand it;*
I'm gonna leave the planet. And I planned it.
But God had a hand in it, commanded.
Dying isn't your prerogative, my dear.
It's important that you live.
And now I'm glad to still be here.

And I'm one of the lucky ones in my illness tribe.
I had a mother who scrimped and saved, to help me survive,
And when my friends left, 'cause they thought misfortune was
 catching,
I had a partner who stuck by my side through everything.

Imagine others alone and undiagnosed,
Begging on the street, unemployed and comatose.
If we had money for research, we could find a cure,
And no one would have to suffer like this anymore!

We're sick and tired of being tired and sick,
And we're gonna keep shouting out LOUD, yeah
We're the Millions Missing, I love my tribe, you make me proud, yeah!

I'm proud of you just for surviving,
just getting through another day and staying alive.
I'm staying alive, you're staying alive,
we're staying alive, just staying alive.

The Color Orange

Driving to work one day, I heard a haunting interview on the radio with a man who was a former hostage. He was imprisoned for months without outside contact. He said, "It was a gray, uninterrupted hell," until one day when a guard left him a magazine to read. He recalled seeing an advertisement with a large orange background that moved him to tears. He said, "You can't imagine the happiness I felt, just seeing the color orange." He added, "I don't see the world the same way anymore. Other people, they don't even see the beauty that's around them. I do."

I understand a little bit of what that hostage went through. During the last ten years I have had a chronic illness that frequently kept me imprisoned in my home. When my symptoms were unendurable, it was the smallest things that kept me going. A tree in bloom outside my window, a craft project I could do in bed, an email from a friend . . . these things were lifelines. I understand how the color orange could get you through another day.

During the first years of my illness, I thought my limited life was rather pathetic. And I thought the tiny things that made me happy were pathetic, too. Everyone else, it seemed, was getting their joy from big, visible accomplishments like getting promoted at work and buying houses. I was getting pleasure from my fuzzy blanket. But soon, my suffering began to teach me to focus my awareness. When I was in severe pain, whatever helped me out of that pain for a moment became suddenly precious, like I was experiencing it for the first time. Later, I thought, *Oh, that's what Buddhist monks work so hard for, to stay awake to the preciousness of things*. I began to think of my life as a forced period of monastic study. That notion restored some of my dignity.

I began to wonder—since we have a world full of things that are capable of inspiring us, why aren't we all happier? Why did that man have to get imprisoned before he realized the life-affirming powers of a color? Why did I have to get sick before I appreciated my fuzzy blanket?

I began to explore my relationship to happiness. What I learned has been invaluable for my self-development. When I looked over my childhood, I realized my family had a bias towards gaining pleasure from fulfilling a duty rather than from enjoying something directly. For instance, we planted peas in Grandfather's garden because his sister Helen liked to eat them when she visited. So, we could speak about Aunt Helen enjoying the peas, but we never mentioned their sweet perfection ourselves. Similarly, clothes shopping was done for practical items only (L.L.Bean for warm jackets, Thom McAn for sturdy shoes). No one in my family went on a vacation. No one bought a car because they thought it looked cool. No wonder I had judgmental views about pleasure.

I trained myself to find new ways of taking in pleasure. I would purposely stop what I was doing, from time to time, and notice things around me, like the taste of my coffee or the iridescent feathers on a hummingbird hovering by. If I realized that I wasn't enjoying an activity, I stopped trying to talk myself into it. For instance, I noticed that I didn't like meditations with deep breathing; they just made me feel irritable. So I stopped. If I got pleasure from something, and it didn't cost anything, I let myself have a lot of it. For instance, I really enjoyed audiobooks, so I downloaded every free Agatha Christie audiobook I could find. I allowed myself to spend countless hours lying down and listening to the stories. It felt like a private luxury allotting myself that much time for pleasure. But without getting sick, I wouldn't have given myself permission to relax and just listen like that.

Children have their priorities straight when it comes to happiness. I find it refreshing to hang out with children because they know a good thing when they see it. Time spent with children reinforced the new beliefs I had acquired about happiness. They, too, understand the joy of fuzzy blankets.

Once I was teaching a bunch of kids how to mix colors with paint. I took a scoop of red paint, and then yellow paint, swirled the two together, and they watched as the color—*gasp!*—changed into orange. The children emitted a quiet "Woooooow" and that wow charged the act of mixing paint with electric excitement. We experimented with adding a little extra red to make a reddish orange that looked like molten lava, and then we added more yellow to make a mango color, and then even more yellow to make a marigold color, and soon we had a whole rainbow of orange patches of paint, spread randomly over the paper. Then they took turns with the paintbrush and painted pictures of dancing fruit and friendly orange bears enthusiastically riding on orange skateboards towards an orange sunset.

And that former hostage, he would have loved our painting party too. I wonder if he still appreciates color the same way, decades later. I like to imagine him, racing through his busy day like everyone else, until a bit of visual beauty stops him in his tracks. A bright purple-red glass of cranberry juice, the gold-white gleam of sunlight on his daughter's hair, the midnight blue of the sky as evening turns into night—these sights would make him pause, just for a moment. And on his face would be the same enigmatic smile as a Buddhist monk sitting down to meditate in robes of orange.

Laila Solaris lives in a tiny house on wheels parked in the beautiful wine country area of California. This house was built because of her need to find a home with fewer environmental toxins. Laila spends most of her time coming up with creative solutions to help her deal with the limitations of her illness. She has also become the full-time caregiver for her partner, who recently had a stroke. The two of them are committed to living a happy life together, no matter what. A video of her reciting the poem "This Rap Is Chronic" can be found in the Video section of the Pillow Writers website, pillowwriters.wordpress.com.

Dawn McReynolds

Just Make Some Art

When your body won't work, and your life seems uncertain . . .
    stop thinking and just make some art.

When your inner sky darkens, and your spirit starts sinking . . .
    stop thinking and just make some art.

When you stare at the page, quite unsure where you're going . . .
    stop thinking and just make some art.

When you're utterly certain, none will want your creation . . .
    stop thinking and just make some art.

When you can't fathom how, your work will be found . . .
    stop thinking and just make some art.

When your heart has laid bare what it needed to say, and you've done what you set out to do . . .
stop thinking,
  wish it well,
    set it loose to fly free,
      and get back to making more art!

Becoming Better

Each day becomes a feat of bravery to battle the mind and coax my spirit to simply show up. To be present. To complete another day.

    There are so many options for quieting the storm within. I could eat sweet food, I could run myself into the ground, or I could be angry with everyone just because. But I know these will only release the emotional and/or physical pain of this breakdown of my body and my active life for a moment and then it will return. Deep down I know there are only two things to do:

> Acceptance will give me peace.
> Actions will give me progress.

But how do I learn to accept this life as it exists in this moment? I don't think it's possible. The only idea that comes to mind is this: Although I may or may not get better, I can still become better. Getting physically better is not fully in my control, whereas becoming better at living this new life is completely in my control.

I can become better at handling fatigue, pain and stress. I can become better at being present, grateful and calm. I can become better at accepting rest as a legitimate activity, and I can become better at making each moment the best it can be, regardless of how I physically feel.

I can become better at choosing to rise.

Dawn McReynolds was a runner, hiker and university academic advisor when her health took an abrupt turn after exposure to toxic mold. Although currently doing better, she lived with ME/CFS for over seven years and in that time rediscovered her passion for creative projects. For Dawn, writing is about the touching of hearts, the meeting of the soul, and the invitation to readers to think about their own lives in new or meaningful ways.

Kelly Littrell

I Fit Here

I am alone again in the blackness. You sleep with ease. Great distance between us, I now amble towards you beneath the cool white sheets. The warmth of your body radiates. I move your arm and lay my troubled head on your bare chest. My stomach against your hip. My willowy right leg curled around yours. My left foot nestled on top of the hairy Hobbit feet I know. Your arm holds me tenderly. Securely. Even in sleep, you gently kiss the top of my head. I am loved. I fit here.

    I can feel your effortless breath and hear your heartbeat. Everywhere that my skin touches yours I am comforted. The intensity of my pain dissipates. Here I find tenderness and understanding. Safety and compassion. There is also great beauty. My own breathing has slowed. I fit here.

    I no longer care how much time passes. My once shallow hungry breathing is deep and sated. Soon every inhalation and exhalation match yours. My troubled mind tranquil. My heart full. My body mended. My dispirited soul returned. I mercifully drift into long-forgotten splendorous sleep. I fit here.

Sun and Moon

Our friend Sun has returned
spreading daylight, warm and clear,
caressing my sleeping girls
who awaken in good cheer.

The twins jump from their beds,
race to sleeping parents near

and with jubilant smiles,
they shout, "Morning's here!"

Bright Sun begins to laugh
as she greets her precious two,
reminded of their special bond,
a friendship old and true.

A happy tiny twosome
start another beautiful day
with a venture to the kitchen.
Daddy's pancakes on the way!

The twins spend their sunny day
in enchantment from their dreams.
But not the stuff of fairy tales,
tall tales, or make believe.

Instead, they venture outside
so friend Sun is not alone,
for this family loves the outdoors
more than Calvin loves his bone.

It's a morning filled with laughter,
giggles throughout the afternoon.
Another day's adventure
promised by the stars and Moon.

Each night Sun and Moon
greet each other in the sky,
a secret stolen moment,
a conspiratorial sigh.

Their journey then continues.
Moon changes place with Sun
watching over the restless twosome
once the dark night has begun.

It starts off with a bathtime
that lasts two hours long.

Mama reads at least a dozen books,
Sun's twins still going strong!

Moon helps by triggering yawns
and next comes the eye rubbing.
Are our tiniest adventurers
giving in to sleep's coming?

Yes! They've fallen sound asleep
in Mama's lap while reading.
Daddy comes to Mama's aid
already hearing the deep breathing.

In their beds they're gently placed.
Mama whispers, "Thank you, Moon."
Back to sleep the parents' race
for Sun will be here all too soon!

Moon's already promising
what fun friend Sun will bring.
Dreaming twins and Moon converse
as tiny snores and grumbles sing.

Moon and Sun then pass in the night.
Sun is excited to have learned
what dear Moon has promised twins
while the Earth has turned and turned.

Calvin the Dog

They look just alike.
I must be seeing double.
Identical preschoolers
can be so much trouble.

At their last tea party,
their movements in tune,

they both sipped their tea.
They both licked their spoons.

And when they giggled,
they both hid their smiles.
But that twinkle in their eyes
could not belie their guile.

Our mama says they're sweet,
as sweet as can be.
"Give them a chance,
then you too will see."

The only thing sweet
from what I can see
is the cantaloupe they drop
on the floor just for me.

Their imaginations run wild,
always roles to play.
Miss Clavell and twelve girls,
Madeline saves the day.

They call me Genevieve.
They towel-dry my shivers.
Apparently, I'm cold.
I fell in the river.

Daddy tells them, "Be nice.
Use kind words when you can."
But then they always call me,
"You grumpy old man!"

Kelly Martin Littrell has had ME/CFS for thirty-five years and lives in Atlanta, Georgia, with her college sweetheart husband and twin daughters. At age twenty, Kelly contracted mononucleosis (caused by the Epstein–Barr virus) at the University of Georgia and never recovered. With the aid of her parents and husband, she transferred to Georgia State and became an event planner, writer, editor and photographer for their College of Law. Fourteen-hour event day crashes and co-conditions forced her to stop working. Kelly and her husband are the proud parents of the loves of their lives, identical twin girls, now in college. Kelly has lived with severe, moderate and mild ME/CFS. Two years ago, she developed long COVID and a very severe overall worsening of all prior conditions. To Kelly and her sister Kimberly (who has Sjogren's syndrome), their friend and Southern Mama, Lynne Martin, has exemplified living with a severe autoimmune disease while maintaining her sarcastic sense of humor. Kelly is also determined to live her best life, no matter her baseline: mild, moderate or severe. This had included her greatest joy, shepherding two daughters on their journey to becoming great adults.

Martin Keogh

It's Like Amnesia

It's like amnesia

Every time
I feel
a smidgen better
I forget I am ill
and rush into the
joy of activity

And again,
I find myself
falling into
the abyss
where fatigue
has no boundary

All these years
later I rush to
the joy of activity

Every single time

This Long-Haul Illness

This long-haul illness
is my jealous lover

He looks over my shoulder
aware of any time I engage
with another person or endeavor

She belittles me in front of others,
demands I always report to her,
follows my every move,
threatens to leave me (Oh, please, please!),
won't let me leave the house alone

When in public he hangs an arm
heavily around my neck,
fat palm over my chest

She always knows who I'm talking to
and is there in a flash if she feels
anything spark inside me

I'm terrified he will find out
I'm imagining another kind of life

I Know I

I know I
will recover

Against all
the evidence
and all the odds
I know this
to be true

My symptoms
will ebb away;
my cells will
regenerate

I will live a life
brimming with
vitality, stamina

and the constitution
of an ox

To not shatter
into a million pieces
each week, month
and year,

I'm compelled
and duty-bound
to hold and trust
this to be true

Martin Keogh is also known as The Missing Neighbor. Along with being a parent of four, and now a grandparent of four, Martin once toured several continents a year as a professional dancer. He lived a full, engaged life. Then one day he was struck by myalgic encephalomyelitis (ME/CFS) that left him mostly homebound and partly bedridden.

Amid the tsunami of symptoms, Martin is granted about twenty minutes a day when he is able to focus. He started using this time to write his reflections about this condition. Turns out that writing twenty minutes a day can turn into a book that people can hold in their hands and hearts. That book is titled *Naked Realities: Living with an Invisible Chronic Illness* and can be found at Amazon or any e-bookstore. Find more of The Missing Neighbor at instagram.com/the_missing_neighbor/reels/.

Trish Loehrer

To the Caterpillar

To my son who is also one of the #MillionsMissing. May you have many beautiful tomorrows.

Yesterday,
    which may have been last month or last year,
my body and legs
did the locomotion to crawl
along the branch of a tree.
Insurmountable Entity that They were,
I scarcely spared a glance for the sky.
There was nothing for me
in that profound void.
I found joy in the grasses,
food in the bark and dirt.
I
    was
        so
            busy
with my surroundings.

On a different yesterday,
    which may have been last week
    or last month,
I awoke to the sun
on my newly formed wings,
delicate and damp.
emerging from the dark cave
in which I had no consciousness
nor any thoughts of emerging.
simply existing
in a shriveled state
while my body
    melted
        away.

Today,
    which may be one of several tomorrows,
I see a vast, unknown sky.
A warmth dries my wings
and nourishes my spirit.
I am fed by the flowers.
Was that actually me
who crawled in the dirt?
Or was that a different being
with their consciousness imposed
upon my new body?

On another tomorrow,
    which will happen when Nature dictates,
I will fly to the skies
    on a long migration
a journey that I
cannot fathom today.
For how can I worry
about tomorrow's tomorrow
when today's sunshine
is so beautiful?

With all my love,
                The Butterfly

Rest in Pieces (a Dialogue)

On my healthless days
No light could touch my eyes
Every sound causing a full collapse.
Period.
Therefore, I rested.
But resting took all of my energy.
Exclamation point!

                                    Tell lungs to fill, then exhale.
                                           Remind heart to beat.
                                                             Chew
                                                              One
                                                              Bite.
                                                              Nap.
                                       Applesauce through a straw.
                                                            Sleep.
                                                         Feel love.

Staying alive was my marathon.
Was I supposed to learn something?
Should I have internalized peacefulness?
Question mark?

                         There was nothing peaceful about that rest;
                               Nothing restful within that quiet.

The passing of a day indistinguishable from a week.
A week from a month.

                                              Resilient. Tenacious.
                                             A body torturing itself.

Hundreds of people over thousands of days
Brought me out of that "rest."
MDs, PhDs, surgeons, researchers,
Nurses, interns, students,
Transporters, technicians, phlebotomists,
Drivers, caretakers, and . . .
Ellipsis

                         Find balance, train eyes, rebuild muscle.
                               Neurons work together again.

In retrospect, it all sounds so exhausting.
In the moment, each win was exhilarating.

> Each one just a set up
> To overcome the setback.
> Full Stop.

I now see those silent days as a mere example;
Semicolon.
Proof that quiet is possible.

> Now that you're standing,
> Return to the quiet
> With a new mindset of rest.

A healthier me (with M.E.)
Now with more spoons
And yet . . .
My striving remains
Level same.

Busyness has been my business.
"Think more." "Do more." "Exist more."

> !!Whoa Stop!!
> <u>It is time</u>
> To learn balance.
> "Do
> *Only*
> What can be
> *Easily*
> Done
> With great peace
> And simplicity of heart"

I am ready.
Question mark
Am I? Are we?

    The "we" of body, mind, heart, and soul.

"I" aka "Little Miss Brain"
Is not doing this on her own.

    We are, as friends, moving forward.

Trish Loehrer is just one of the #MillionsMissing. Everywhere she goes, she bumps into people with ME or other chronic illnesses. They inspire her daily to keep fighting, to show up authentically, and to "lift as you climb." She thanks the nuns of the Carmelite Monastery in Carmel, California, for the inspiration of "Do only what can be easily done with great peace and simplicity of heart."

Jenny M.

The Endless Wait

Today the last of the snow on Mt. Crestone's peak has finally melted, announcing midsummer. It's one of the ways I know time is actually passing at a normal rate. The endless waiting I do as an ME patient makes it seem as though time is simultaneously standing still and traveling at warp speed. Days last for eternities but years are gone with the snap of a finger.

I occasionally experienced this feeling before I got sick, but it has been exponentially heightened by the fact that I am either sitting in a chair or lying in bed for twenty-three hours every day. My daily routine does nothing to mark the passage of time. I live the same day over and over. Only the face in my mirror tells me that I have been surviving this illness for twenty-nine years.

The never-ending waiting infects the present moment with urgency despite there being nothing on my schedule. Like a burrowing insect, it is an ever-present irritation. It begins to spread through my body, causing anxiety, frustration and confusion. I use breathwork as a balm. I try to soothe the angst with meditation and music. Since breathwork, meditation and listening to music all take energy, I must rest after each "activity." Thus, the interminable waiting ensues again. Even when I manage to do a little more, like take a short walk outside, my enjoyment of the activity is often marred by the feeling of wishing time would move more quickly.

Remember the feeling of being in school, waiting anxiously for the bell to ring out freedom for another afternoon? There were times when I stared at that clock, willing its hands to move. I couldn't believe time could creep by so slowly. I breathed hard; my body grew hot with frustration. I lost focus and could not attend to my lesson. I tried telekinesis to move those clock hands. Until they finally ticked away, I was stuck with that burning desire to hear the bell. Imagine that feeling never going away because the thing you are waiting for never comes.

I am waiting for a return to living instead of surviving. I am waiting for a chance to get up from the chair I rest in all day, to go outside and do more than sit in a different chair. I don't want to just look at the mountains; I want to climb them. I want to pick up a violin again. I want to catch my own dinner in a river again. I want to lose myself in a book again, but I can't. I am stuck—trapped by an illness very few people know about. I am waiting for a cure, and I very much doubt it's coming in my lifetime. I fully expect to feel the burning desire for life, the agony of endless waiting until the day I die.

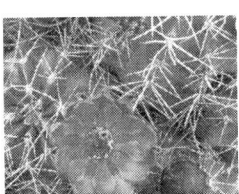

Jenny M. was an avid athlete, musician and voracious reader as a teenager before she got sick. ME robbed her of the health necessary to do these activities and live a normal life. Twenty-nine years after falling ill, Jenny still struggles to accept the limitations imposed on her by ME. She lives in Colorado where she is cared for by her parents. She finds inspiration in the beauty of the high desert, which often shows up in her writing and art.

M. S. Marquart

My Local Life

Once a day, I open the window and press my nose against the screen, breathe in the outdoor air, feel the sunlight warming my face.
I promised my dad I would try to do this, and every day there's a new scene.

I smell the rain, the ice, the springtime freshness, the summer heat.
I watch the trees change color, drop their leaves, whiten with snow, turn green again.
I listen to the sounds of New York City, with subway trains setting the rhythm, punctuated by sirens and children giggling and shrieking.
Cold winds howl between the buildings until an ice cream truck circles and baby birds beg.

One day, dogs bark frantic hellos, jumping to urgently greet old friends.
One day, birds swoop to the ground for a kicking, flapping, chirping dust bath.
One day, an arborist rises into the aqua sky, trimming bare branches with exquisite expertise.
One day, a toddler sobs, inconsolable over a broken cookie, sparking nostalgia over kid-size problems.
One day, a delivery person rolls a clattering cart overflowing with holiday packages for my neighbors.
One day, children play Times Square, counting down and cheering Happy New Year, then laughing and starting again.
One day, the first flowers of the year suddenly appear, living sunshine, yellow against the dirt.
So much life in my little neighborhood.

The stimuli send me back to bed, blackout curtains closed. No lights, muted sounds. My body overwhelmed.
Before long COVID that became myalgic encephalomyelitis, my daily

city views spanned blocks and boroughs and parks and rivers. The Central Park Zoo, the Metropolitan Opera, Cafe Lalo.
My local life like the opening montage of a movie.

Three years on, my local life is whatever my senses glimpse out the window.
The months slip by in once-daily scenes.
I am one of the ME #MillionsMissing.

The Bench

Shivering on a wooden bench in the dark,
I wait.

The smell of plants surrounds me.
Rats run past my feet,
Unavoidable in a New York City garden at night.

5 minutes pass.
My strength hasn't returned; I can't walk again yet.
I finish one podcast episode and start the next.

20 minutes pass.
My body is still too fatigued to stand.
I try anyway and collapse back onto the bench.
My head spins. My heart races.
My eardrums throb. My legs shake.
I start a new podcast episode, I play a game on my phone.
I wonder when I'll be able to get home.
It's cold and my jacket is thin.
I feel the icy wind and stare into the night.

My boss says my documented disabilities are no reason to work from home.
It doesn't matter that my work is done on a computer,
That everyone I supervise works remotely,
That each time I go to the office my health deteriorates.

I spent my day doing virtual meetings and emails.
No reason to be there in person except for my boss's command.
And now I can't get home.
My employer boasts about its anti-racism, anti-ableism,
workplace wellness, inclusion, social justice.
This week, a colleague was shocked at how different I look;
another gave me her arm to walk back to my office from the bathroom.
I live 5 blocks away from my job.
This is the second bench I've rested on during this journey.

The bench is around the corner from my apartment building's
    entrance.
I can see my kitchen window.
It might as well be a million miles away.
My stomach squeezes. My bladder throbs.
My heart pounds. My eyes ache.
My shivers intensify until I'm shaking.

It's been 30 minutes.
My husband is out; I can't ask him to come downstairs and get me.
I text a friend, embarrassed but daring to hope.

She responds she's on the way!
I sob from relief, my tears chilling my cheeks.
I taste salt in my mouth.
I force myself to stop before she arrives.
My breath hiccups until I get it under control.
If I can't control my legs at least I can control this.
It's hard enough to have to ask for help just to walk around a corner
because I'm stuck on a bench.

The relief releases the panic that has been building all night.
My blood buzzes.
What if this is irreversible?
Have I lost my ability to walk?
What else is going to happen to my body?
I block out the fears before my friend arrives.

She walks up through the shadows, gives me a hug,
Picks up my bag, loops her arm into mine.

She supports me as I tap tap along with my cane.
She walks very slowly to match my pace.
She talks about other things to take my mind off of this.
She says she cares.
She makes me laugh.
She makes us hot tea when we arrive.
I warm my hands on the mug and smell the comforting spices.
My body slowly stops shaking.
I feel so grateful to her and so angry to be in this position of needing rescue
because of a lack of work accommodations.

Power

> *I'm sorry to hear that your doctor has written a letter stating that due to your long COVID and ME/CFS disabilities, your health will be severely and irreversibly damaged by coming into the office. You may have done this job remotely for years, but now you need to come in three days a week.*

What may I do from home, and what must I do in the office my job provides?
Answer emails; work on spreadsheets; read articles and guides?
Talk on the phone; join web meetings; collaborate with remote colleagues nationwide?
Facilitate virtual trainings; draft presentation slides?
My boss decides.

When coming to the office permanently harms my health, what is worth making me sick?
Being available just in case my boss needs to pop in for something quick?
Needing all bodies in the office to justify the rent expense uptick?
Being physically closer to participate in the vicious internal politics?

Sitting at a desk for any VIP's boot that needs a lick?
My boss has the power to pick.

How much will my health deteriorate?
Will I never be able to go have coffee with friends; never take my husband on a date?
Never travel to see my aging parents again, who live in another state?
Never stargaze; never lie on a beach; never watch the spring flowers in the park regenerate?
Never earn another degree; never learn an instrument; never artistically create?
Never achieve my dreams; never have a day when my health feels great?
My boss controls my fate.

Might I live or might I die?
My boss decides.

M. S. Marquart is a disabled, mixed race Asian American poet who writes about life with long COVID and myalgic encephalomyelitis (ME/CFS). She is grateful to #MEAction and the Pillow Writers for the opportunity to be in community when able to join, and to be welcomed without judgment and with deep empathy and kindness. Visit more of her work at msmarquart.com.

Mary Quigley McGowan

Elizabeth

I met Elizabeth only once, briefly, in a bleak hospital day room in 2006. She told me about her life.

Elizabeth was wraith-like, her gracious brown eyes buried deep in a ravaged face. Tethered to a huge oxygen tank, she had been lugging herself back and forwards and up and down stairs to demonstrate that she was well enough to go home. I could see through this pretence; I suspected that the medics could, too, but they agreed to discharge her.

Afterwards, she lowered herself delicately next to me, every breath an almighty struggle. In retrospect, sounding a little too clever, I said, "You must be desperate to get home. I can see the effort you put into that—you're really not ok, are you?"

"Naw, but I hate hoaspi'als. Whit ur ye in fur?" she replied slowly, over a series of breaths so shallow they seemed to originate and terminate in her throat, making her speech almost unrecognisable.

"I've developed some scary heart problem they're looking into."

"Dinnae worry hen, they'll look efter ye. Whit is it that ye dae?" she asked in her staccato Scottish rasp.

Feeling painfully aware of my relative good fortune, I said, "I'm a lawyer and I've got three wee ones, the youngest only two. How did you end up here?"

"Ach hen, I've been a smoker a' ma days and it's caught up wi' me. I weesht there was a pink pill, save a'body the bother."

Her reply shocked me, and I moved a bit closer to inquire how this could possibly be the case. "Really? I can see how hard it is for you, but is it really that bad? Surely, you've got loads of time to please yourself?"

"Naw."

"What, you don't watch the telly, or read a book, or get stuck into crosswords?" I said, betraying exactly what I'd do if I had the chance.

"Naw."

"Maybe just watching the seasons pass?"

"Naw."

"Long lie-ins," I persisted.

"Naw."

"You must have visitors popping in to chat?"

"Naw, jist me henk," she gasped, wearily but kindly.

Utterly incredulous, I finally asked the one open question with which I maybe ought to have led. "How is life for you? Is there anything you enjoy?"

"Naw," she wheezed sadly, and without a trace of exasperation or self-pity. "Evry day is jist . . ." and she trailed off, desperately trying to catch a breath, knowing she would never again catch a break.

Feeling helpless, I said simply, "I'm so very sorry for you. I can't possibly imagine what you're going through."

"Aye," she replied, looking directly at me, her eyes fathomless wells of wisdom and suffering,

"I daresay ye cannae." And, with that, she rose unsteadily and trudged off, her hospital companion clanking behind her.

Elizabeth was alone, her whole life consumed by drawing her next suffocated breath. No colour, no meaning, no joy. A wretched existence saturated by unbearable pain and fear.

Elizabeth told me about her life; she foretold mine.

How Are You Feeling?

I feel like I'm discovering hidden nooks and crannies in a deep, dark pit of suffering. Occasionally, I stumble upon a ladder, but after a rung or two, it gives way and the pit becomes deeper, its sides more sheer and unassailable. Meanwhile, the rescue helicopter of medical science is grounded on a sticky platform of psychobabble, ego and scandalous politics. Such doctors as are obliged to venture close peer down at me, shrugging their shoulders and shouting helpful advice: "Work within your capabilities." "Don't fight your body." "It's possible to relax too much." Sometimes they try to throw me a ladder, but it's too short, or made of gossamer. Then they leave me to it. Alone. In silence. In the dark.

Or

"I'm fine, thanks for asking."

What difference does it make?

Mary Quigley McGowan lives in a Scottish village. The view from her bedroom window is spectacular, which is fortunate as, largely, it has been her only view for more than ten years. She became unwell in 2006 after a series of chest infections and a hill walk. Initially, she worked on and necessarily off as a solicitor with her three young children foremost in her thoughts and decisions. Over the years her health deteriorated and she replaced her LLB (Hons) law degree and diploma in professional legal practice (Dip LP NP) with ME/CFS, postural orthostatic tachycardia syndrome (POTS) and mast cell activation syndrome (MCAS). Joining Pillow Writers has added a further affliction: Joyful Imposter Syndrome in the company of such exceptionally talented writers. Now, she can generally be found in front of a screen cheering on her beloved Celtic Football Club. Other musings by Mary may be found in her blog *Ordinary Miracles* at merrydholl.wordpress.com.

Sarah Sundermeyer

What I (Almost) Tell My Friends

Oh, I'm doing fine // I haven't been myself in years // I think getting a dog could fix me // Won't you move closer? // It's lonely out here // I'm fighting my body again // On bad days I have "flame brain" and "the zonks" // Do you think I should tell my doctor? // I wonder if they believe me // I think I could have changed it if I knew // Illness has made me selfish // I'm still waiting on new research // I'm so sick of being sick // I'm just trucking along like always // Who designed the world like this? // I forgot to take my meds // I hate that there are consequences for everything // Two hours with a friend and I'm out like a light // I'm proud of myself for trying // I wish I had appreciated my health before it came crashing down // I don't feel young anymore // I think my mom is worried about me // I barely remember what it feels like to jump on a trampoline // I wish I could explain what it feels like in my body right now // I wish I could be like I used to // Why can't I be like I used to?

Sarah Sundermeyer is a queer white educator and artist living in Oakland, California. Since contracting ME/CFS two years ago, she has found solace in knitting, painting and chats with disabled pals. Pillow Writers is her first step toward practicing more vulnerability about disability through writing.

Mary Gessert

Robin's Only Desire

The horse and rider flew down the course, galloping like a centaur outrunning the devil itself. Robin switched off the television and slowly rose from the couch. Just two years ago that would have been them. They didn't usually watch equine events anymore as it was too painful a reminder of what could have been.

Robin's mother had insisted that the hard-won scholarship to Stanford not be wasted, even though all Robin wanted was a spot on the United States Equestrian Team. "College is a waste of time, Mom! I won't be able to put in the hours training if I have to study for exams." Having ridden since the age of five, Robin was addicted to the speed, power, risk and beauty of galloping cross country and flying over obstacles. Back on the ground, they felt diminished and invalid.

In the end, to keep the peace, Robin agreed to go. It seemed nearly too good to be true when they found Charles Caffrey, an ex-Olympian rider, with a more than able mount, nine-year-old warmblood Thoroughbred cross, Captain, to lease in return for stable and exercise work. The ranch even had an efficiency apartment above the tack room, only twenty minutes from campus.

One Friday night, they went out to a hole-in-the-wall restaurant with a few friends, had some tepid chicken noodle soup, and ended up sick with salmonella food poisoning. After three days of living in the bathroom and wishing they would die or get better, they pretty much recovered. But after two weeks, Robin noticed that the achy joints and fatigue still lingered, and they were having trouble sleeping. Too busy with school, work and training to worry about it, they pushed through each day. Robin's single-minded focus was on qualifying, and when speeding around the arena or across the surrounding golden hills on Captain, they forgot their aches and pains.

Exactly a week after their amazing performance at the Blenheim Spring Classic in San Juan Capistrano, Robin rolled the stall door open to find Captain stretched out on his side, groaning in agony. "Shit! Chuck! Captain's down and colicking!" They ran for the office, dialing the vet's office with trembling fingers. Fumbling with the keys to the safe, Chuck opened it and grabbed a syringe and a bottle of xylazine. As hard as Chuck and Robin tried, they couldn't get the poor animal on his feet, and Robin sat crying and stroking Captain's satiny neck as Chuck injected the painkiller. An hour later, despite the veterinarian's quick response, the horse was dead, a twisted gut, too far gone for surgery. Robin wouldn't leave the horse's side until the knacker came to pick up his body. "How can we just throw him in the landfill? He was my friend and partner! We loved each other! We were a team!" they sobbed. Heartbroken, Robin stayed in the apartment, mostly lying in bed, face to the wall, for two weeks. Final exams came and went. Chuck brought food and tried to say all the right things, but he finally lost his patience and hired another hand. No degree, no trainer, no horse, no home, no energy, no dreams, "I knew it was too good to be true," thought Robin rereading, for the umpteenth time, the letter congratulating them on being short-listed for the 2024 Olympic team, heading for Versailles.

The Party

Robin is easily overlooked in a crowded room. They are quiet and unassuming, dressed in unripped jeans and a plain blue T-shirt. Their clean chin-length black hair tends toward ringlets, framing a symmetrical, serious face. But if you catch their dark eyes, a glowing smile rises spontaneously. There is something there that is cautious but friendly, shy perhaps. Robin holds a half-full glass, one leg jiggling, and one hand unconsciously rubbing Ranger's long hound ears.

Jody had invited all of their AA group to the party, and they wanted to be supportive. It's difficult to socialize with able-bodied folks when you're young and your disabilities are invisible. Getting dressed and driving the short two miles to Jody's apartment had used up most of Robin's reserve. A normal day was spent in bed or on the couch with resident bunny Basil, reading, writing, or watching BritBox crime shows. Robin, ashamed, sometimes has a twinge of jealousy when they see someone in a wheelchair being treated with kind deference.

Ever the gracious hostess, Jody brought Robin a small plate filled with savory nibblers and fruit.

"Oh, thank you," said Robin, standing up to take the offering.

"I couldn't remember if you have any dietary restrictions."

"No, it's fine. Thank you so much!"

Robin took the plate and looked at the slice of summer sausage perched on a cracker. They are vegetarian, but didn't want to offend Jody. The plate trembled in Robin's hand.

"Are you alright?" asked Jody.

"Just a little tired," Robin replied and sat back down.

Jody moved on. They wondered why they had even bothered to come. It had only been twenty minutes and Robin had planned to stay for at least an hour so as not to appear rude. Mission aborted once again, they put the plate under the chair, gave the dog one last pat as it scarfed down the snacks, and snuck out the back door.

The Battery

Rachel woke up with an aching head, her heart racing like it was going to explode. After twenty long years struggling to recover, her memory remained foggy, and her vision was blocked by shadowy rings. Her limbs felt like they were sunk in quicksand. The new battery, which should have recharged her body while she slept, was low once more.

There would be no tiger in her tank this morning. She sat up slowly, trying to trick her mind into wakefulness, but her slowly spinning thoughts wouldn't clear. The latest technology was supposed to allow her to care for herself, but every time it was the same sad story. The system would work for a few days, then would fail to charge past fifteen percent. Just two days ago they had done some adjustments, and she had been able to take a shower. She couldn't pretend anymore that she wanted to live like this. If she had been an appliance, they would have ordered a replacement. But her body was past its use by date and the recycling centers and junk yards didn't have anything compatible. And then there were the supply chain issues. So, she lay aboard her bed in her homebound cage and looked out the window, watching a crow pecking at the carrots in her neighbor's garden. She was thirsty and needed to pee. What a filthy, rotten existence. When the phone rang, it was the nurse. They explained that they had found another charger to try. Her hopes soared, and the crow took flight.

Mary Gessert is an avid reader but is new to creative writing. In her first life she was a veterinarian. After contracting Q Fever from an infected goat herd, she developed ME, which forced her to sell her busy practice and leave her beloved Wisconsin farm. For a few years she worked for the U.S. Department of Agriculture doing inspections and drafting reports. But when the travel became too exhausting, and the weekends too short to recover, she had to retire early. Her brother and sister, both storytellers, encouraged her to write for fun. Her counselor suggested she write to manage her grief. Then she discovered Pillow Writers, an incredibly inspiring group of authors. She treasures their weekly sharing of poetry and stories.

In her second piece, "Who You Are," Manu Vargas Fernández expresses the impact her mother and family have had on her well-being. An essay by her mother, Gloria Lucía Fernández Gutierrez, follows. Gloria explores what it is like to have an adult daughter with ME who is living at home again.

Manu Vargas Fernández

The Angry Dog

Every now and then, no matter if it's day or night, I'm visited by a big angry dog. When I hear him coming, I hide under the bed, feeling his breathing close to me. The dog sticks his snout out, desperately trying to reach me. It's terrifying. The last time I thought he was dead because I got out of bed and kicked and hit him until he left. I didn't like hearing him cry, but I couldn't have stayed under the bed all my life. I had to make a decision.

The dog was back and, as always, I went under the bed. However, this time it was different. Instead of pushing myself against the corner of the wall, I slowly approached him and offered him my hand to smell. To my surprise, the dog's anxiety decreased and he came to smell my hand. Very slowly, I dared to touch his head and pet him affectionately. The dog threw himself on the floor as a sign of trust, so little by little I encouraged myself to get up.

The dog wasn't as big as I imagined, and since I petted him, he stopped barking so loudly. In any case, when he comes back now, it's not a pleasant visit. He breathes down my neck all the time as if he is waiting for the moment to attack again. I had to get used to it, and I understand that I can't get him out again by kicking him. The dog is still there, kept calm only by caresses and goodwill, and although his presence is not pleasant, at least I can bear his company until he decides to leave.

From time to time the dog comes back. I don't know where he comes from or where he goes after he visits me. What I do know is that I can't attack him because the more I attack him, the more he attacks me back and the longer his visit becomes. I've learned that when he comes, the only thing I can do is to pet him and be very patient until he leaves. This dog is more like me than I would like, and it really is like he is a part of me. Sometimes he comes, sometimes he goes, but he is always with me.

Who You Are

You have looked after me for six months without saying anything, without complaining, without thinking for a moment that I am interrupting your life. My father has done it, too, in his own way, but you have had to give yourself over to my care in a devout way: "Mommy, bring me a glass of water and the pill." "Mommy, help me to make the bed." "Serve some tea for my friend Paula who is visiting." To all these requests you only answer "Yes, my love" and, in the most diligent way, you help me whatever my need or desire.

In this family of four—my father, my brother, me and you—you are like a beacon of light that guides us in the darkness of life: Without realizing it, you maintain our day-to-day, you hold the threads that pull us and get us out of an existence that could be miserable, or without exaggeration, very dull and soulless.

Thinking about my own death has led me to think about the deaths of each of you. I asked my dad what he would do if you died first. He told me that he would sell this farm and divide the inheritance between each of his two children. Then he would go live in an apartment in the city and that "everyone would fend for themselves."

"Fend for themselves as best they can?" I asked him. Before he could answer, I told him that I couldn't fend for myself. I needed to be cared for in order to survive. He told me that it wasn't his problem, that you are you, but that he is him and that I would have to manage to live as best I could, that I would surely find the strength to do so.

He definitely doesn't understand that I can't live alone in these circumstances; he doesn't understand the seriousness of this matter. *Is it a man's problem?* I thought. How can it be that he hasn't noticed the difficulties I'm in if, like you, he's had to witness the same six months of my life since I got COVID-19? It must be a man's thing; it seems like they live in a different orbit. Although what he thinks makes me a little sad, I'm grateful that he's still here.

I also asked you what you would do if my father died first. You told me that you would stay on this farm. You couldn't imagine living anywhere else. This land where you have lived for almost twenty years has become very important to you. Every tree, every bird and animal that enjoys the existence of this piece of enclosed land is admired and loved by you. You live here happily, like someone who has connected with a being greater than themselves and can sit peacefully in a chair to observe the small movements around them. Your smile shows it, and the way you respectfully treat this place makes it seem like you are always grateful. I admire your ability to contemplate and experience the beauty around you. But what I admire most about you is your strength, your fortitude, and your ability to understand the big things in life. You understand that someone gets sick (like me), that someone dies, that life goes on with what it is at the present moment.

The rest of us would be devastated if you were the first to die. My father's answer proves it; my brother must not have even thought of this possibility. I have asked God many times for this not to happen, that I be the first one to die. I want this not only so that no one else would have to deal with me, but because I would not be able to bear the immense emotional pain that your loss would cause me. It is simple and drastic at the same time: If you die, I die. I have told you this, too, and you just smile at me like someone who doesn't believe it or doesn't want to give it much importance. Not as if you think that what I am talking about is nonsense, but precisely as someone who knows that even if that happened, life would also go on. Your trees, your birds and animals would continue their vital course, no matter what.

This morning I heard you walking back and forth, paying close attention to all the details that are needed to keep a house standing:

sweeping the floor, cleaning the bathrooms like every day, making rice and cooking. Then I knew that you were reading in a quiet place in the house because there was no more hustle and bustle. I thought, *There is my mother*, and I felt a great relief. Suddenly I felt a great terror: *One day she may not be here anymore*. The only thing that calmed me was the feeling that you are here today, and that I am too, and that we are together in this difficulty, that you are with me, that I am very lucky. I am not alone.

Manu Vargas Fernández is a Colombian artist and filmmaker with over twenty years of experience. She has been suffering from ME/CFS for ten years, and in the last two and a half years she has had to leave her job as a teacher for young people and adults in various communities in her country due to the illness. Since then, she has dedicated her time to writing short stories and creating short videos about her illness and other subjects she is passionate about.

Gloria Lucía Fernández Gutierrez, mother of Manu Vargas Fernández, shares her thoughts on living with her daughter who has ME.

Gloria Lucía Fernández Gutierrez

Here and Now

My eldest daughter, Manu, is suffering from ME/CFS. She has been sick for ten years, but almost three years ago her condition worsened due to a COVID-19 infection. Manu was completely bedridden for a year, needing my help twenty-four seven. She, an independent woman of forty, had to return to live with me and her father, as she needed all our support to survive. The one who was once an artist, creative, traveler and athlete now depended on us for her most intimate needs, struggling every day to walk from her room to the living room, and from the living room to the kitchen to feed herself. Thank God, two and a half years after COVID, she has improved a lot. She is now much more functional, and although she has not gotten her life back and keeps struggling with the disease, now at least she can dedicate her days to what she likes most: art, her friends and her cat Rosa.

What is it like to live with someone affected by myalgic encephalomyelitis (ME)? What does it mean to know the reality of chronic fatigue syndrome (CFS)? Although it doesn't sound original when I say it, having the presence of ME/CFS in your daily life is like living with a ghost.

In its earliest presentation, and sometimes for years, it does not show a specific face; it has no name; it is not recognized by anyone. My daughter had appointments with everyone from allopathic doctors to alternative medicine doctors, then tried medications and infusions. She tried everything from swimming to yoga, from psychiatrists to shamans. And meanwhile, the ghost gained more and more ground. Its presence devoured her routines, dreams, work and circle of friends.

Months and even years passed. Until finally, after a series of diagnoses, or perhaps by having some luck and finding a doctor who has heard about it, it was possible to give that ghost a name. It was possible to say: "Hey, you're not a ghost. You have a face. You are an organic entity. You are not depression. You are not something psychosomatic. You exist. You are concrete and, unfortunately, there are millions in the world who also suffer from you. I don't fear you so much anymore. You have a name."

But then we realized that ME/CFS is more nebulous, more ethereal than you think. There are an infinite number of symptoms; the patient's condition can change from one hour to the next; the slightest effort can cause a relapse, and depression likes to be associated with the condition. Mysteriously, the person we love can lose their voice or suffer every time they eat. They may not sleep well or may suffer from inexplicable pains.

Nevertheless, little by little, I was able to accept this ghostly reality. This is life here and now; this is what it is. I don't look towards any future. I just keep moving through every morning, every afternoon, every night. I am happy with each improvement without longing for it to be definitive, and I witness each negative symptom without fearing that it is permanent.

Here and now, here and now, here and now.

And although my daughter's life (and ours) has changed radically, I do not allow the ghost of ME/CFS to create new fearsome ghosts: the ghost of what there was, of what it has done; the ghost of what could have been and was not; the ghost of the future; my daughter's ghost ten, fifteen, twenty, thirty years ago.

Because for me, this daughter of today is not a ghost. This is my daughter who is very sick. She is this person I love: concrete, contradictory, fragile and brave. My daughter exists, here and now, just as she is. No matter what these circumstances are or how they change, her essence, her light, remains and is not harmed by any ghost, not even that of ME/CFS.

 **Gloria Lucía Fernández Gutierrez** is the mother of Manu Vargas Fernández. She was born in Colombia and lives in the countryside with her husband and daughter on a beautiful mountain near the city of Medellín called Santa Elena. She enjoys taking care of her garden, reading many books, meditating, chatting with her children, her partner, and walking with her two cats: Fermín and Rosa. A lover of words and what can be shared through them, she sometimes likes to write short texts that reflect what she has in her heart.

Sol Howard

Ten Haiku
Extracts from 2020–2023

bedbound
always chasing
crumbs

fading self . . .
the mirror too far
from my bed

night air
crisp and mossy and . . .
closing the window

days old sweat
sad sticking to me
reading love stories

laughter
in the other room
they're all together

turning to the side
soap on my back
I explain my illness again

weak smile
my father brings up chestnuts
and peels them for me

fat robin
picking at seeds
in between poems

long shadows
missing
so much of myself

earplugs
I hear my heart beating
trying its best

More

a huge miracle
by a small bottle
revived
but not cured
welcomed back
to the land of the living—
a little bit
a glimpse
not clubbing
or restaurants
or holidays
or work
but sitting in the wheelchair

watching the poplars
straight and tall
and shimmering
i move with a sticky shadow
under my heart
like a dead bird
i can't get rid of:
past me
in endless darkness
years of longing
for other people
other places
other stories
staring
in the dark
losing
losing
losing
always more

how do i
stop hurting
for what they lived through?
how do i stop seeing them
in all the mirrors, worrying
they will reach through
and grab me again
how do i stop
the whispers late at night
—just one bad covid
a few bad crashes
and you'll return
to that abyss—
i wait for my breath
to even out
tell myself
i'm here now

i take a bath
alone for the first time
strong enough to hop in
and enjoy the heat
to soap myself up
and sing
the waves dance with me
we celebrate
living
a little bit
more.

Sol Howard is a French and English non-binary twenty-eight-year-old. They live in the Paris suburbs with their parents who care for them. Sol enjoys visits from their sister, girlfriend and friends who all live elsewhere. After studying sociology, they gave guided tours, did play work with disabled children, and put on a poetry exhibition in collaboration with a photographer. They decided to pursue their passion professionally and were on the cusp of applying for a master's degree in creative writing when they got ill with ME. For three years they were too severe to write anything but haiku. They want to be well enough to write at least one novel and fill it with trans and crip characters. Find them at @sick.haiku on Instagram.

CJ Janzen

A Hero's Journey

When I was well, at the drop of a hat I would hop into my car and take a holiday. I was free to galivant wherever my heart led. I had no worries, no fears, and I was only constrained by time and money. I took a last-minute trip to Cuba. Sometimes I'd drive eight hours to visit my family in Chicago.

After developing myalgic encephalomyelitis (ME), almost everything changed. Planning a trip now takes years to save up for because living on a disability check means that I must eke out a dollar here and a dollar there. I don't just count dollars, even the pennies matter. Some months are so lean that there isn't enough food to eat, so taking a holiday feels like a pipe dream, but with planning and persistence, I made it happen.

The week before my intrepid adventuring, I rested in bed as much as I could, trying to build up a small reserve of energy and praying it would be just enough to get me safely where I wanted to go. My energy reserve was already partially depleted by showering and packing the car the day of my adventure. The happy butterflies, the fear of the trek ahead, and the anticipation of the pain and joy that were about to transpire made me tremble.

Getting out of the city and onto the highway mentally overstimulated me, leaving me nervous and jittery. But then I hit the open road and was free to breathe and believe that this was happening! The drive eventually became calming and monotonous, but the surcease of fear made me more aware of the mounting pain searing into my body.

The hum of the tires and my ever-decreasing gas gauge told me I was making progress, and yet my mind vacillated between anticipation and trepidation: Family. Pain. Fun. Brain Fog.

I reveled in the scenery along the highway. I was denied this pleasure for so long because I had been trapped in my bed by illness and wave after wave of COVID-19. I listened to my audiobook to distract me from some of the ratcheting levels of aching, seizing and stabbing pains.

As I got closer to my destination and uncharted territory, my ever-increasing brain fog obscured my ability to think clearly. I was wholly dependent on Siri's voice in the car, but she was speaking to a faulty operator. Her voice guided me turn by turn, and somehow, I still got turned around. After more than three hours, I was almost to my bio-uncle and aunt's home. I was starting to get nervous, as I had never met her before discovering my biological family three years before. Would she accept me like the rest of the family had? My ever-increasing brain fog obscured my ability to think clearly, and I was wholly . . .

At last, I arrived! I did it! My family came running to the car and their arms enfolded me. I was trembling in the driver's seat. The elation of seeing my family after three years coursed through me. Without shame, I cried tears of joy.

My legs collapsed as I tried to get out of the car. My family helped me into my wheelchair. I wanted to sit with my family, talk to them, and *be* with my family. Instead, I had to lose precious time with them and rest. Without rest, my brain won't work, my speech is slurred, and words are ephemeral wisps that I can no longer find or use coherently. The broken shards of my body screamed at me, so sleep, rest and pain-killing meds all came before my family.

During my visit, I basked in the joy of being surrounded by my family. I only had a few hours before my traitorous body forced me to be excluded from this normal life. Merely sitting up in the living room with the energy of my family's conversation, the too-bright light, the cacophony of sound, overwhelming scents of normal living—these scalded my body and pierced my brain. I tried to participate in the conversation, but this ripped away at the minimal energy I gleaned from my recent rest. I could no longer take it. I retreated into bed, and into the blessed oblivion of sleep, if I was lucky. My Uncle Ken rushed to my side and helped me into my wheelchair with a look of serious concern on his face, but I lied, and laughed it off . . . as usual. "I'm fine, really. I'm just tired!"

We shared laughter, music, and stories, and made new memories to treasure. But I knew I would forget most of this. My ability to retain the memories of these experiences has always been my nemesis. The longer I am away from home, my pain ratchets up to level four, five, six, seven, eight. But my joy abounds. I can never experience the best parts of life without an equal measure of pain. I must always "pay to play," and I don't regret it. My eyes were sparkling with laughter; my heart overflowed with uncontainable love.

Then, I faced the daunting drive home. It was the most dangerous part of my journey because I was no longer carried by the anticipation of connection to family. I faced the stark reality that it would likely take me months to recover from this adventure. But I was perfectly okay with that; I knew the risks.

I returned home to my four walls, to my support workers who aid me with my daily living, to the bed that adjusts to provide me with the least amount of pain possible. I gleefully reunited with Abbey the flabby tabby with her purring and warmth, and her eccentric goofiness that makes me laugh. Then, I finally started recovering from my trip.

My life is limited, but it's not bad, and this makes me thankful to my family who made this trip so incredibly precious. I'm grateful for the waving fields of wheat, at being able to view the mighty Detroit River again as I crossed over the Ambassador Bridge, and yes, even to be amongst the bustling traffic of life as it harkens back to the days I used to drive these roads behind the wheel of a big rig, back in my trucking days. All of these things made me smile along the way. I am grateful for the ability to provide others with what I could afford to give, and for the fine weather and decent roads which made the trip as painless as possible. I hoped my way home would be safe and without snags, that I would be smart and know when to pull off when it became too hard.

With everything I do in life there is pain and suffering in equal measure, but I choose to live joyously within the tempest of adversity.

Choose to Live Joyously Within the Tempest of Adversity

Do you remember the Monty Python song, "Always Look on the Bright Side of Life"? The chorus starts like this:

> Always look on the bright side of life
> *(Whistle)*
> Always look on the light side of life
> *(Whistle)*

When I think of this song, not only does it make me smile, but I also consider it a great piece of advice!

I was once told there are two ways to live life and the difference is only the changing of a single letter. You can choose to be "bitter" or "better."

As a child, I tended more toward bitter. I was angry and resentful, as I didn't have the coping skills to recognise and appreciate the joy in my life as I do now.

Have you gone through a tough time in life? Have you been bullied, experienced the death of a loved one, confronted a health crisis, been through a divorce, suffered abuse? No one gets through life unscathed by injury or sorrow.

I was physically, sexually and mentally abused as a child. At the same time, I watched my mom deteriorate over thirteen years from cancer until she finally passed when I was sixteen. I am currently winning a lifetime battle with alcoholism, and as I lay here writing this, I am 98 percent bed bound, coping with three autoimmune illnesses. These are just the highlights of "CJ's life sucks," but believe me, there's even more hurt and anguish beneath the surface.

I ask you *not* to feel sorry for me because everything I have survived has turned me into the person I am now, and though I wouldn't wish my childhood on my worst enemy, I am stronger, more loving, and compassionate because of it. I had to tap into that strength when I came down with myalgic encephalomyelitis in 2012. I had the choice to curl up in a ball, give up and die, or to find a new way of living. Everything that I was was ripped away from me.

I couldn't drink, I couldn't work, and friends abandoned me because I could no longer come out to play. Instead of giving into despair, I changed my mindset from dwelling on what I couldn't do and started to think about what I *could* do. With that in mind, I developed my own quotation that I live by: "Choose to live joyously within the tempest of adversity."

Think of the worst day of your life. I bet there was at least one beautiful moment during that day that didn't take even a second to appreciate. Perhaps it was the scent of a bouquet of flowers at the hospital. Or, maybe you noticed the sun sparkling off the waves of a river, or perhaps it was as simple as the mouthwatering first bite of a chocolate bar, and yet you weren't able to appreciate it because you were failing to cope at that moment. By recognizing and appreciating the smallest of joys, those moments can help lift our flagging spirits on even the worst days.

Recently, my father had a medical emergency that required me to pack up his home of fifty years, and with the help of many, get him moved into a long-term care facility near me. In spite of crying and feeling completely overwhelmed, I took time to visit my favorite haunts, reconnect with friends, make new friends, and even visit my mother's grave. I took the time to appreciate these things. Even though this was one of the worst times of my life, I still felt loved, supported, and surrounded by beauty. I worked hard to find a reason to be grateful every day, and that's what got me through it all.

When life hits you and knocks you to your knees, then *try*. It's not always easy, but look for those small gifts, those little treasures that can help you recenter and strengthen you for what you must endure that day. By choosing to live joyously within the tempest of adversity, that attitude of gratitude can change your life for the better.

I once knew a woman who no matter what meal was offered to her, it was either too hot, too cold, not enough or too much. She always chose to see the world through negative eyes. It made my heart sad to see a person who was only happy when she was unhappy. I wish I could have shared with her my approach to adversity—"Choose to live joyously within the tempest of adversity." Find your own joy and choose better over bitter. Don't forget to sing a little, and to always look on the bright side of life (*whistle*).

CJ Janzen is The Singing Speaker, an international speaker, author, certified Chief Well-Being Officer, and the creator and producer of {dis}ABILITY Unleashed. Though living with myalgic encephalomyelitis (ME) leaves CJ 80–90 percent bedbound most days, CJ Janzen doesn't let that stop xyr from achieving xyr dreams. CJ teaches others how to become Joyful Resilient through the use of stories and songs as xe provides the skills needed to help xyr audiences start again after a major life change. ME changed xyr life, but CJ refuses to let it rule xyr life any longer!

Emily Wright

Dizzy Girls

When a spell comes on,
as unwelcome as the
condition that fuels it,
I try to think of the
merry-go-round, the teacups—
of clasping hands with
a friend, leaning back,
and letting our feet
make the afternoon blur.

I try to remember
a time when I craved
this feeling—sought it out—
a time when I was
desperate for my
world to move, to make
me a spinning top,
a vortex of color and
giggles and calliope notes.

When I grieve that
far-gone "normal,"
I try to think of those
bright-eyed, gilded ponies
whose lives are an
infinite, stable circle,
who inspire imagination,
who embody the fantastic,
who run extraordinary.

 **Emily Wright** is an educator, writer and researcher based in Southern California. She hopes for a day when she can walk her two dogs again.

Set in postwar 1950s Scotland, the following is an excerpt from a longer story. It was inspired by conversations that took place during Pillow Writers meetings. More of "The Inn at Lathones" can be found on the Pillow Writers website, pillowwriters.wordpress.com.

Emma Parsons

The Inn at Lathones

"Dear God, Smith, did you see that?"

"Err, yes, Sir."

"What in God's name . . . ?"

"I understand it's one of the locals, Sir." Smith kept his eyes on the road but passed a bulldog-clipped collection of papers to the Commodore in the back seat. "I believe you'll gather from the notes that it's a Mr. Campbell, Sir."

"On a bike."

"As you say, Sir, on a bike."

"In a wet suit."

"One can only hope it's nothing more sinister, Sir."

"But we're miles from the coast."

"Only about five miles north, Sir, as the crow flies. Or nearly six as the Scottish man cycles." Smith's permanent boredom occasionally inclined him towards inappropriate levity.

"Quite so." Commodore Cholmondeley-Smythe sighed. He was not planning on enjoying this latest secondment. Firstly, the Scottish weather didn't agree with him and secondly, there were the warnings he'd been given about this Smith fellow, bit of a subversive apparently. All "Yes, Sir," and "As you say, Sir" on the outside, but there was something supercilious about the fellow. Minor public school.

Scholarship boy. Commodore Cholmondeley-Smythe cheered himself with this belittling thought. Then he remembered the oversized local cycling past in the too-small wet suit and his heart sank again. "Where is the nearest place in this godforsaken place to get a drink?"

"We could try the Inn at Lathones, Sir?"

Smith began the laborious process of a three-point turn in a too big car in a too small road, narrowly avoiding an Austin 7 that was taking a nearby bend with unnecessary speed.

When Smith and the Commodore arrived, the Austin 7 was parked chaotically in the gravel car park of the Inn at Lathones. Years of training meant that Smith automatically parked his vehicle so that he was able to examine the stationary Austin 7 in his rearview mirrors. A habit that made him despair at himself. Those few duplicitous years of war had, he reflected, left him utterly unfit for civilian life. Always suspicious, always alert, even in the most tediously dull of places like the car park of the Inn at Lathones. Still, leopards don't change their spots, so, as he opened the rear door to decant the Commodore, he took a complete inventory of the Austin, its driver and the passenger. The driver, he noted with some surprise, was a young woman, an appealing mix of blondish hair and apparent good humour who was carefully applying a rather startling shade of Yardley lipstick. Her passenger looked on patiently with a damp tongue lolling out of slightly yellowing teeth, constrained enthusiasm seeping from every pore. Smith was still watching as the driver and her companion left the car and headed towards the Inn. The driver's clothing was much more practical than the view of her face had led Smith to imagine was likely. The words *sturdy* and *durable* swam into his mind. He imagined her on the lawn of a dour Scottish castle, sensible brown boots making dents in a dew-covered lawn, readying herself for the start of grouse season.

"C'mon, Lallo." She patted her tweed-coated thigh as she hurried towards the door, needlessly, because her canine companion was already at her side.

"What are you staring at, Smith?" The Commodore's clipped tones broke through any thoughts Smith was having about lipstick, tweed thighs and even hounds.

"Sorry, Sir, I'll just gather the papers. Doesn't do to leave these things lying around."

"Quite so, quite so." Commodore Cholmondeley-Smythe strode efficiently across the gravel yard and towards the public house, anticipating a fine single malt. Smith carefully stashed the buff folders, with CONFIDENTIAL rather comically stamped upon them, into his leather briefcase before following the Commodore into the Inn.

Smith assumed that the Commodore hadn't noticed Campbell's black bicycle leant against the wall. Smith hadn't warmed to this latest superior sent here to oversee what he very much considered to be his radar station. Nobody of real value was ever sent this far away from Westminster. The work was tedious and largely pointless. Smith was fully aware that his own posting had been by way of punishment. They had a tendency to send him people of rank and limited ability to keep them out of harm's way. His latest boss appeared to be very much of this mould. Still early days. Smith girded his loins, ducked his head, and entered the gloomy but welcoming public bar of the Inn at Lathones.

He was surprised to note that, presumably by accident rather than design, his disappointing Commodore had chosen the perfect table. A small round table in the corner, at the back, slightly secluded behind a beam, two chairs both with their backs to a wall, providing views of the bar, the door, and out through the window. Better still, two glasses of whisky had already been placed upon the beer-stained table.

"Cheers." Smith gratefully raised his glance in what was not intended to be a sarcastic salute.

"Cheers. Took the liberty of ordering you a spot of lunch." The Commodore ignored Smith's polite expressions of gratitude. "Did you notice?" The Commodore nodded at the black lifeless rubber suit hung on a hook behind the bar. Smith had noticed. He'd also noticed that the dog lying happily on the rug in front of the unlit fire appeared to have misplaced its owner.

Campbell was seated at the bar. Nursing a still full pint glass, he was adequately if unconventionally dressed. The barman stood near him, slowly drying a glass—half wipe to the left, half wipe to the right. Largely ineffectual but peaceful. Neither of them spoke. The dog stirred as the smell of cold beef wafted by encased between spectacularly white slices of thick, soft, freshly baked bread.

"There you go, gentlemen. Two beef sandwiches. Will you be wanting anything else, now?" The substantial landlady smiled, as did both Smith and the Commodore. None of them were wearing lipstick.

"Marvellous."

"Marvellous."

"Marvellous."

"It was this or an egg roll. Took the liberty of choosing for you."

Smith, mid-mouthful, was unable to reply but his approbation of the Commodore's choice was unmistakable. The atmosphere between the two gentlemen thawed, and they ate in perfectly happy but watchful silence.

"I'll be off, then." Campbell placed his suddenly empty glass decisively on the bar. The barman nodded; Campbell nodded. The dog twitched. Smith and the Commodore watched. They watched Campbell exit the door, they watched him walk past the window into the car park, and then they watched him continue his journey along the road back past the Inn, not on his black bicycle but in a blue Austin 7.

The Commodore surprised Smith by looking at him and raising an eyebrow.

"Curious," said the Commodore.

"Quite," said Smith. "He's left his wetsuit."

"All finished, gentlemen?" The landlady bustled from out of the back to remove their crumb-less plates. "Can I tempt you with anything else?"

"Sadly, no. Must get going. Things to do, things to do. Devil finds work for idle hands and all that. We were just saying, you've a particularly fine Austin in your car park."

"Henrietta?" The practised hands of the landlady simultaneously stacked the plates with one hand and wiped the table with the other.

"The owner?"

"Lord bless you, no. That's the name of the car."

"Who does own her?" Smith decided to take a more direct approach than that allowed by the irritating avuncular manner of the Commodore.

"Who owns Henrietta?" The landlady paused. The plates in her right hand held motionless, the cloth in her left temporarily stationary. She looked upwards towards the beam, searching for an answer. "Do you know, I've not the faintest notion." And with that she bustled off, calling over her shoulder, "You'll settle your bill at the bar, will you, gentlemen?"

Against his more prosaic nature, the Commodore had finally admitted defeat and allowed his wife and children to name his own car; therefore, he was possibly the least surprised of the two, but the idea you could know the name of a car and not know the name of the owner mystified them both. Their mutual perplexity served as a cue for them to leave.

"My treat, Smith."

"Really, Sir, terribly kind of you."

"Not at all, not at all."

Their preparations for departure explained why neither of them noticed the direction that the next person to enter the Inn had arrived from.

The Commodore watched with amusement the effect on Smith as a tweed-clad figure strode into the bar.

It wasn't just Smith who reacted to her entry. The whole bar changed. Lallo rose from the hearth and took her impressive bulk for a tail-waggly enthusiastic greeting, the bar man wiped his glass with a vigour one would previously have thought was beyond his ability, and the Commodore's "hail fellow well met" persona became more pronounced than ever. There was just a general air of joy. The Commodore having settled their account, they left the newly jovial Inn with differing degrees of reluctance. The Commodore surprised Smith by requesting that they return to the Radar Station. In his experience, his superiors were always keen to be returned as swiftly as possible to the comparative luxury of the hotel. There was, after all, very little to see. But he turned the car left out of the car park, and back they headed.

"Nothing about her in your notes on the locals, Smith?"

"No, Sir. Commodore Beauchamp said, and I'm quoting here, 'not to bother with the women folk.'"

Commodore Cholmondeley-Smythe snorted. "Commodore Beauchamp is a damn fool. Comes from having a name nobody can pronounce I 'spect."

Smith didn't yet know Commodore Cholmondeley-Smythe well enough to be aware that he was joking. He squinted at him in the rearview mirror.

"Yes, Sir." There was a lot more that Smith could have said about the inadequacies of Commodore Beauchamp, but experience as well as a naturally secretive nature inclined him to hold his tongue.

The Radar Station was an unprepossessing building. Damp moss clung to the damper roof of a pitiful single-story Operations Room. Vital during the war, new technology had rendered it all but obsolete, and whatever the Cherry Report had concluded about the unfit state of Britain's RADAR system in a nuclear age, budgetary constraints meant that change had largely ignored this particular area of Fife. Astonished that his latest superior officer had chosen to visit twice in one day, Smith took himself to the little kitchenette and offered the Commodore a brew.

Entering his office with two freshly made cups of tea, Smith cast around for somewhere to sit. The Commodore had requisitioned his seat and his desk and, much more improbably, a series of buff folders from one of the filing cabinets. Smith knew from personal experience that the guest chair had long since lost the sort of integrity that a chair requires in order to be properly considered a chair. He leant awkwardly against the least damp wall. The Commodore didn't look up, but he gestured with his fountain pen. "We'll be needing new furniture. Couple of nice leather armchairs for the other room, too. No point being miserable. See to it, will you, Smith?"

No point in being miserable was a novel concept to Smith. He tried contemplating it for a bit, tossing it into the gloomier corners of his mind, but it didn't stick. "No point in filling in a furniture request form" was the thought that lingered, but it gave him something to do. Something that didn't involve leaning awkwardly against a wall trying on the Commodore's outlandish positivity for size.

"I'll speak to buildings maintenance myself. Get me a line, would you?" Any form of building maintenance had eluded Smith and all preceding commodores since Smith had arrived. Smith had kept the building largely watertight with a hammer, some tacks, and his own endeavours. The consequence of getting the Commodore a line, however, was that a buildings team was due to arrive "first thing in the morning" to "get the place shipshape." Smith admired the Commodore's optimism. An admiration for optimism that continued as he watched the Commodore stamp URGENT on their furniture requisition form.

During the drive back to St. Andrews, Smith surprised himself by hoping the Commodore would invite him for supper. If it surprised Afternoon Smith, it would have absolutely astonished Morning Smith, but there was something about his new Commodore that had, over the course of their day together, captivated his interest. To put it bluntly, he'd started entertaining the notion that Commodore Cholmondeley-Smythe wasn't quite as dumb as he looked.

Assuming that his passenger wouldn't notice, Smith had taken a slight detour in order to see if Campbell had collected his bicycle or if it was still resting outside the Inn. "See that Campbell has come back for his bike then," remarked the Commodore.

"Or someone has."

"Quite. Henrietta, perhaps?" The Commodore laughed at his own joke. "Good idea to detour, by the way. Intelligence gathering is never in vain. Can't help noticing the dossier on the locals is a bit on the light side. Nobody of the fairer sex, that sort of thing."

"Yes, Sir, Commodore Beauchamp . . ."

"Quite, quite, Beauchamp. Yes, indeed. You said." Glancing in the mirror, Smith saw the Commodore's moustachioed lip purse in anger. Briefly, but it was there. "But you have suspicions of your own. Unofficially?"

"Not really, Sir. Both officially and unofficially. I can't say anything has struck me as suspicious about any of the locals."

"Dear God, man, I've been here less than twenty-four hours and I've seen a wet suit on a bicycle, a car that isn't owned by anyone, a barman who can't dry glasses, and a pub offering egg rolls for lunch. Egg rolls! You still want to tell me there's nothing suspicious about the place?"

"Put like that, Sir."

"Quite."

"In my defense, Sir, I've never before been to the Inn at Lathones."

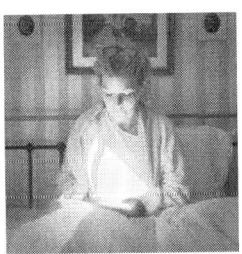 **Emma Parsons** hosts Soft Pillows and runs the Pillow Writers website and BlueSky account. She writes long-form fiction as a means of escape from the unbearable physical constraints of ME/CFS. Pillow Writer meetings have been a great source of joy, friendship, inspiration and encouragement, for which she will be forever thankful.

Monique S. Simón

If I Open My Eyes

If I open my eyes,
the darkness will return.

I will see no one
has come to see me

as I am

still alive
still dreaming

in the wake of my affliction

of sunshine
and laughter

of lavender
and peonies
teasing my nostrils . . .

In the light behind closed eyes,
I run my fingers
carefree
yet gentle

across blossoming fields
of beautiful possibility . . .
If I open my eyes,
the darkness will return.

Only to fill my vision
with withering flower
devoid of sunlight
fragrant no more
inside the locked door
with the missing key.

Beauty Struck

Yes, The Beauty is making a show of it.
But not all at once.

I caught up with her in the springtime—
when she was sporting early blooms.
Spring colors,
    accented by fresh, flirty lime greens
An array of flowers,
    preening as she put on quite the scene.

Ah, then Act II—the passing of the baton looms
When the display changes actors
And the light of day factors
In a show of zinnias and jennies
And an encore of pink peonies.

Yes, The Beauty is making a show of it.
She has me on my knees—
Struck down like a dunce,
I pay homage,
By pulling weeds.

Clean Linens

I've tried Tide, All, and Arm & Hammer
But nothing's been washing out these
Leaving-me blues

The sheets are 800 thread count Solid Egyptian cotton
But the fiber's gone to pieces
Of memories
Rinsed free of your touch

Mama always said you gotta change sheets regular
Wash 'em good and long in hot water
On account of those skin-eating things

But now all I got is this tumbling death song
Spinning circles around My fresh dried eyes
    "What? No, Ma. He's working late!"

So late, the clock's long broke . . .
Mama's losing memories
And the pup's peed on the rug

I got nothing but reminiscing
And my feet in your oversized house shoes
But I'mma hang on

To these first sheets we sullied
Though they're ruined now
With the smell of lavender

Monique S. Simón has lived with ME/CFS for more than thirty years. A former professor, department head and education programs developer, she sustained her career through a relentless "push/crash" cycle until illness forced her into disability retirement. An award-winning writer, she has been published in *Better Than Starbucks*, *Whisky Blot*, *Tiny Seed Literary Journal*, Health Affairs' *Health Narratives Poetry Series*, and anthologies. Her novel-in-progress was excerpted and illustrated in BWIA's in-flight magazine (500,000+ circulation).

Now, Monique is the Founding Editor of Wildflower Wisdoms™ | Living ME, a magazine dedicated to energy-limiting chronic illnesses (ELCI). Through storytelling, art and expressive arts facilitation, she uplifts the resilience of those navigating chronic illness. Her work, infused with warmth and wildflower wisdom, reminds readers that even when life demands stillness, growth is always possible. View more of her work at wildflowerwisdoms.com.

Emrrys Oliver

I've Been Distant

I've been distant lately . . . when I see people I care about messaged me.
Instead of feeling comforted, I feel afraid.

I'm afraid that I'll say the wrong thing,
that I'll hurt people, that I'll do the wrong thing and lose them,
that I've already done the wrong thing because
I was too scared to message.

I don't know how to cope with how overwhelming this is right now,
how overwhelming it's been for so long.

I know it's not fair to put that on people I care about.
I'm distant because I don't know how to be a good friend.

Because I don't know how to *be* right now.

I've been distant lately because I don't have the energy to reach out.
I'm struggling so much to eat, to drink, to use the washroom, to rest.

I wish that not being able to do things made forcing myself to *not* do things easier.
I wish the pain of wanting to visit with friends and not being able to,
even if I had the opportunity, didn't hurt so much.
To ration out the things that make me happy . . . in this many days,
I'll get to do a fun thing. In this many days, I'll get to leave these walls.

I've been distant lately because if I push people away and they leave because of me,
then it's not another thing that's been taken away from me.

If people don't care about me, then it's one less person who would be sad if I were gone.
Then it's one less person I would have to stay alive for.

I've been distant from myself. I've been distant because I'm lonely. I'm distant because I miss you. I'm distant because I miss me.

To Be Recited

I love poems that can be recited.

Read back and forth, between friends or lovers,

So much meaning in words not our own, and yet it speaks between our souls.

When words reflect feelings, not social etiquette,

When eyes meet, deep and tearful.

A soul fully seen. A heart full, or broken.

A poem crosses the bridges, that we cannot.

                      A poem crosses bridges, that we cannot.

                      A soul fully seen. A heart full, or broken.

                      When eyes meet, deep and tearful.

                      When words reflect feelings, not social etiquette,

So much meaning in words not our own, and yet it speaks between our souls.

                      Read back and forth, between friends or lovers,

                      I love poems that can be recited.

You're There

When my anxiety spirals,
I can feel myself getting pulled further in—
my giant puppy snores like an old man and I snap out of it for a moment.

I like hearing snores, well mostly.
To giggle a little, at how funny you are
snoring like my grandfather in a living room chair.

To not even realise I'm picking at my skin,
As nails bite into skin and make it bleed.
Moving from one spot to the next—

When the hand I forgot was on my shoulder twitches
as my mom dreams next to me.
When I put my hand against her back so I can feel her breathe.
To know she's there—makes existing a little less terrifying.

The things that remind me loved ones are there.
To see a message from people I love, that they're awake too.
To send them a message saying I'm struggling.
Sometimes they respond right away, sometimes
I leave a letter on their metaphorical doorstep,
Knowing that, somewhere in the same world, they will send a letter in return.

That the darkness of my mind, that I face every evening,
Is not something I face alone.

 **Emrrys Oliver** is a non-binary person in Alberta, Canada. They write poetry, fiction, songs and create in all mediums of art. They create accessible jewelry such as wire art to hold finger joints due to hypermobility and ear cuffs to hold ear plugs. Although their paintings have been shown in community spaces, they are now too ill to paint and currently channel their creativity into writing.

Emrrys became ill with ME in 2016, and it developed into severe/very severe ME/CFS by 2019. At age nineteen, Emryys is the youngest member of the Pillow Writers. Emrrys is an active and valued member of the group, assisting with technical issues and co-leading the Pillow Writers tea parties. Emrrys is a disability and LGBTQ+ advocate, helping educate their city and those around them to help improve the lives of others.

The print edition, ebook and audiobook of *Near-Life Experiences: The Pillow Writers Anthology, Issue 2* are available at amazon.com.

For more writing by the Pillow Writers, please visit pillowwriters.wordpress.com.

For more events, including salon readings by the Pillow Writers, please visit meaction.net.

Laurence Brangea, the cover artist, is French and lives in Paris with her husband and two children. She got the flu when she was forty and never recovered. One year later, she was diagnosed with ME/CFS, a chronic, complex postviral illness. Laurence was a human resources advisor at the French Bank. Laurence is disabled, functioning at about thirty-five percent, and continues to learn, read, paint watercolors and spend time with her animals (donkeys and dogs) in her countryside home.

Printed in Dunstable, United Kingdom